As fast as she could, Polly con___
twisted and turned, and there was s___
Confused now, Polly was beginning to tire. Removing the
shawl from her head, she sank down on a wooden step in
front of a deserted-looking building.

There sure ain't much of anybody livin' back here, she
thought. *I ain't seen another soul since I passed that donkey.*

Suddenly two large, black boots appeared in front of her.
Slowly she raised her head and looked at the man who was
in them. Polly's face turned white, and she moved as close
as she could to the building. A bandit! Polly knew a bandit
when she saw one. The man was dressed in a black shirt and
black pants, and had black hair and a mustache. Even the
eyes peering down at her were like pieces of coal in his
tanned face. Mutely, Polly held out the bag that contained
her remaining *centavos*.

ACROSS THE BORDER

by Arleta Richardson

CHARIOT
FAMILY
PUBLISHING
A DIVISION OF COOK COMMUNICATIONS

Chariot Books™ is an imprint of Chariot Family Publishing
Cook Communications, Colorado Springs, Colorado 80918
Cook Communications, Paris, Ontario
Kingsway Communications, Eastbourne, England

ACROSS THE BORDER
© 1996 by Arleta Richardson

First Printing, 1996
Printed in the United States of America

00 99 98 97 96 5 4 3 2 1

Library of Congress Cataloging-in-Publication Data
Richardson, Arleta.
Across the border / by Arleta Richardson.
p.   cm.–(The orphans' journey; bk. 4)
Summary: Through prayer, thirteen-year-old Ethan meets the challenges of
moving with his adopted family to a homestead in Mexico.
ISBN 0-7814-0193-3
[1. Orphans–Fiction. 2. Christian life–Fiction. 3. Mexico–Fiction.] I. Title. II.
Series: Richardson, Arleta. Orphans' journey ; bk.4.
PZ7.R3942Ac   1996
[Fic]–dc20

Contents

Dedicated to
the 23 grandchildren and 33 great-grandchildren
of John and Jennie Green,
the inspiration for the Orphan's Journey series.

Introduction

Of the thousands of children who were placed in midwestern farm homes and small communities between 1854 and 1929, remarkably little has been written. The Orphan Train Heritage Society, based in Arkansas, has collected valuable information about those years from the children or their relatives. Many orphans have been reluctant to discuss their experiences, while others speak with deep appreciation of their adopted homes.

It was inevitable that some children would be placed in the care of people who regarded them as extra workers for the farm or business, without regard for their spiritual or emotional needs. Some reported cruel treatment that led to their removal from the home or impelled the children to run away. Many others stayed in situations that were less than perfect, and through their experience became strong, self-reliant adults.

Such was the case for the real "Ethan Cooper." Reflecting on his life after he reached his nineties, he recalled long hours of hard work and harsh discipline, minimal schooling, and few times of fun and childish activity. Yet his attitude was always, "I had a home. I learned a lot. I'm a better person for it." There is no doubt that Ethan's strong faith in God was the anchor that held him through those years.

Arleta Richardson
1996

DECISIONS

Ethan, Polly said to tell you that dinner's ready."

The boy nodded without turning to look at his sister. "I heard the bell."

Alice leaned against the fence beside him and looked out over the fields. "What do you see out there?"

"Work. All the stuff we planted and have to reap in a few months." He shifted against the fence post, and the letter in his overall pocket crackled. He needed to make up his mind about that letter, but it wasn't easy.

Ethan knew every word that was there and reread it in his mind, half-listening to Alice's chatter as they walked toward the house.

> *Dear Ethan,*
> *I have some exciting news! As soon as the*
> *harvest is in, Papa is letting me go to Kansas to*

*school! Will you ask your father if you can come
too? We can room together and work for our
board.*

The letter was from Ethan's friend Bert. He remembered
the wet spring day four years before when he had met the
cheerful, freckle-faced boy. Ma had died, and Ethan, Alice,
Simon, and Will had been sent to Briarlane Christian
Children's Home, the county orphanage. Bert had taken it
upon himself to shepherd Ethan through the difficult way of
life an orphanage offered. When the opportunity came for
children to be put on the Orphan Train, Bert and all the
Coopers had been among those selected, and the boys had
stuck together. One by one the children were left in small
towns and communities across the country until only the
Coopers and Bert remained on the train. To their delight,
all of them were adopted in Willow Creek, Nebraska.

Bert went to live with a happy young couple, Carl and
Hannah Boncoeur.

"Matron was right when she said the Lord had just the
right place for all of us," he said. "He sure found a great
home for me."

Ethan had not been so sure about the reception his
family had received. He had tried to answer Alice's
questions about their new parents.

"Do you think they want us, Ethan?"

"Of course they do. They wouldn't have sent for us if
they didn't."

But, Ethan concluded to himself, perhaps Chad and

Manda Rush hadn't realized how many four children at once would be.

In time, however, they had become a family, together with Frances, an older daughter who had been adopted by the Rushes from Briarlane several years before. Three years ago Chad had moved them all to a homestead in South Dakota. Life there had not been easy, Ethan thought as he looked at the big house surrounded by cottonwood trees. He'd worked every daylight hour along with Luke and Henry, the two hired hands who had come with them. Chad was known among his acquaintances as a "hard man," successful, and relentless in his pursuit of land and stock. He expected as much of his help, including Ethan, as he did of himself.

Nevertheless, Ethan had earned Chad's grudging respect by his refusal to quit when things were hard. The boy felt that he "belonged" and that he was fulfilling his promise to Ma to look after his younger sister and brothers.

Polly opened the screen door as Alice and Ethan came up the steps. "How come you're lollygaggin' over the fence when dinner's on the table?" she scolded. "You waiting for me to bring it out to you?"

She sounded fierce, but Polly was kindness itself when it came to any of the children. No longer considered "hired help," Polly was a full member of the family. Her elderly mother had died the year before, and she had no place to go back to even if she'd had a mind to return to Nebraska—which she did not. Manda needed her to raise this raft of young 'uns, and Polly knew her duty when she saw it.

The dining room the children entered was well furnished, with a big window looking out over Cottonwood Creek. The creek was a river in size, a fact discovered soon after their arrival when floods caused it to creep dangerously close to the house. For most of the year the water ran smoothly, and it was a safe place for the younger children to play.

The rest of the family was already gathered around the table, and Ethan and Alice took their places with the others. Chad bowed his head to pray.

"O Lord, we thank Thee for this food and for the health to enjoy it. May we be ever grateful for Thy bounty. Amen."

"School this afternoon," Frances announced as they began to eat. "Simon, arithmetic before your organ lesson. Will, reading and spelling. Alice, we will be sewing. You have yesterday's seam to take out. It's much too crooked."

This information was met with groans and sighs from the three students.

"It's only a doll dress," Alice protested. "Who's going to notice it?"

"I am. And the Lord will. We do our best on anything we attempt."

Ethan grinned as he remembered Matron back at Briarlane telling him that the Lord cared how he made his bed. It had been a comfortable feeling to know that the Lord was interested in the little things of his life. Alice would find it so, too, he was sure.

Simon would have preferred the organ lesson first, or

better yet, in place of arithmetic. But past experience had taught him that any such suggestion would be met with a lecture, so he nodded his head and went on with his dinner. Seven-year-old Will looked appealingly at his mother, but in matters of schooling, Frances was in charge, and Manda wasn't going to rescue him.

Frances at eighteen was a lovely young lady with wavy brown hair and a pleasant face. She loved to teach the children, and in another year, she thought, she would like to apply for a teaching position in the little town of Winner, just east of them. It would mean staying in town during the winter when the weather was harsh. This, she knew, would not please her father, and for that reason she had not yet approached him on the subject.

Ethan took a deep breath and told Chad about Bert's plan. To his surprise, his father didn't answer with a flat no, but thought it over in silence for some time.

"You are thirteen now, Ethan," he said finally. "You know that at sixteen you're free to do as you like without permission. You've been a good hand on the farm, and Simon isn't old enough to take your place. Why do you think you need to go to school?"

Ethan didn't want to say that he looked forward to spending time with his friend Bert, so he answered, "I want to get a good education. Even if I'm going to be a rancher the rest of my life, I need to learn all I can."

"You've finished your eighth reader with Frances, and you can cipher through the twelves. Do you think you need more than that?"

Ethan couldn't think of a reasonable answer, so he remained silent.

"You're a responsible boy," Chad said at last. "You make up your mind what you should do. The decision is totally yours."

The answer should have made Ethan happy, but it didn't. Back at work in the barn, he talked it over with Henry.

"I know Chad doesn't think I should go. If I decide to leave, he won't like it. Why doesn't he just tell me no?"

"You're old enough to think for yourself," Henry told him. "You have to decide whether you can live with the consequences. One of 'em is sure to be that Chad won't like it. Have you prayed about it?"

"Yeah, but I don't hear the Lord telling me what to do."

Luke had been listening to the conversation. Now he voiced his opinion. "I don't hold much with the Lord speaking to people, but I found out that if I make up my mind to do something, and I keep feeling uneasy about it, I probably better not do it. When it's the right thing, you feel sort of comfortable with it."

Ethan thought that over as he worked in the field. He didn't feel comfortable about it, but he couldn't understand why. He'd worked hard and done his best for four years. Chad admitted that he had been capable and faithful. He had received his schooling in the evenings and during the winter days when they were shut in. As required for all Orphan Train children, Ethan had been given religious training. Whenever possible the family went into the town of Winner for church services. The rest of the time they worshiped together at home. His adoptive parents had fulfilled all the terms of the written contract. Why, then, was Chad reluctant to give Ethan permission to go away to school?

By supper time Ethan had decided that he would finish out the summer's work, and, directly after the harvest, leave for Kansas. He pushed away the thought that he might be making a mistake. After all, Simon was as old now as Ethan had been when he started working on the farm in Willow Creek. They could get along without him. In the fall, he would announce to the family that he was going away to school.

But at the supper table, Chad had an announcement of his own.

"I've had word from my brother George that he plans to stake a claim in the state of Wyoming. That means he can't manage the Willow Creek property any longer, and he wants to know what I will do with it. I've decided to sell the house and the section it sits on and lease the other five sections for the time being. I'll have to go back to hold a public sale. Henry and Ethan will go with me."

Having delivered that lengthy speech, Chad resumed his meal, not seeming to notice the stunned silence around the table. Manda was pale, Frances looked stricken. The younger children ate silently, aware that something important was being discussed, but not sure what it was all about.

Finally Frances spoke. "Papa! Sell the house in Willow Creek? I thought we were going back there to live."

"We're not."

"You are going to sell all the livestock and machinery, Chad? . . . And our home?"

"*This* is our home, Manda. You had everything shipped out here that you wanted for the new house. It wouldn't be practical to move animals and farm equipment this far."

As far as Chad was concerned, the matter was settled. He continued eating calmly, and nothing more was said. A heavy silence fell on the room.

"You could cut the clouds in there with a knife." Polly returned from serving the cake to the family and made her report to Henry and Luke in the kitchen. "You'd think he'd threatened to move 'em all across the country again by the looks on their faces. I thought Manda was beginning to like this place."

"That was her home in Nebraska. Her friends were there," Henry said. "I'm not surprised that she'd grieve over it. You wouldn't think Chad would break it to 'em like that."

"It's just what I'd expect him to do." Polly forked a generous slice of cake onto each man's plate. "If he told Manda when they were alone, he'd get the sharp edge of her tongue. There's safety in numbers, they say." She chewed reflectively on her dessert. "'Course, there's no guarantee he won't get it anyway, once the family is in bed. Not that it will change anything. They've both mellowed a lot since the children came on that Orphan Train, but some things die awful hard. Wantin' to do everything your way is one of 'em."

As Polly washed her dishes and cleaned up the kitchen,

she thought back to the first day they had seen this house being moved by teams of oxen toward the foundation on which it now stood. Manda had been disappointed to learn that she wouldn't have a home built to her specifications, but would have to adopt a large two-storied house that someone else had abandoned.

Polly looked around her kitchen with satisfaction. It had turned out well. The whole house was nicely decorated and comfortably furnished with the things Manda had enjoyed in the Nebraska home. Lilacs and roses bloomed under her care. Her family of five children was well dressed, and her household ran smoothly under her direction. No, Polly didn't understand it. Why should Manda be upset about not returning to Willow Creek?

Manda was quick to tell her when she asked. "My friends. A closer town to shop in. And I suppose I would like to have been asked if I ever wanted to go back before he made up his mind.

"I know I shouldn't complain. I have all my family around me, and a good home. Chad has always provided a comfortable living for us. I just never thought I'd leave for good the place where I grew up."

"Why don't you make the trip back with them?" Polly suggested. "You could have a nice visit with Lydia."

Manda shook her head. "I couldn't leave you and Frances with the garden to put in and the children to watch for. I wouldn't enjoy myself."

The matter seemed to be settled, and Chad set about the business of making sale notices.

PUBLIC SALE

Having sold my farm, I have decided to have a cleaning-out sale at my place joining the town of Willow Creek on

FRIDAY, JUNE 10, 1911 - Commencing at 11 o'clock

15 HORSES AND MULES

1 bay team of mares, ages 6 and 11, weight 2900; 1 team of black mares, age 6, weight 2600; 1 team of gray mares, ages 11 and 12, weight 2800; 1 bay gelding, age 5, weight 1100; 4 mules, age 2, weight 900; 2 mules, 1 year old.

25 HEAD OF CATTLE

20 high-grade Holsteins, 2 years old; 3 fresh; 2 grade bulls.

65 HEAD OF HOGS

15 Jersey red brood sows, good grade.
50 stock hogs weighing about 200 lbs.

FARM MACHINERY, ETC.

2 Deering binders, 3 McCormick mowers, 1 McCormick rake, 2 drags, 3 riding plows, 1 gang disc plow, 1 Dain alfalfa hay stacker, 1 hay sweep, 2 corn planters, 3 walking cultivators, 2 riding cultivators, 3 wagons, 2 hay racks, 1 two-row Sattley, 4 sets double harness, 1 single harness, 1 New Empire cream separator, 200 bushels Early Kerson oats, 15 tons alfalfa hay, 8 dozen full-blooded Silver Wyandotte chickens.

TERMS: All sums $10 and under, cash. On sums over $10, 12 months time will be given on bankable paper, drawing 10 per cent interest.

FREE LUNCH AT NOON

CHAD RUSH

COL. O. V. KENASTON,
Auctioneer

E.R. JOHNSON,
Clerk

Chad read the notice over with satisfaction. This sale would bring in more than enough cash for the plans he had. And he still possessed 3,200 acres of good land in Nebraska. He was confident about his decision. If he listened to the womenfolk, they would be as poor as church mice.

ALICE GOES
VISITING

Alice wandered down to the river and sat on a log, dangling her feet in the water. There were no lessons this morning because Frances was working with Manda. Simon and Will were in the field with Luke, and Polly was boiling water for the jam and jelly they would make that afternoon.

She could be sewing, but since that was her least favorite thing to do, she put it off until Frances insisted that she get it out. There wasn't much time to sit and do nothing.

A number of small stones lay at her feet, and she absent-mindedly arranged them into the shape of a doll house. She outlined a living room and set several odd-looking pieces of rock to serve as furniture. Next she added a kitchen. When a noise made her look up, she watched two squirrels chasing each other until they disappeared.

Across the river was the Rosebud Indian Reservation. Although many of the Indians had been over to work for

Chad, and she knew some of them by name, Alice never had been to their village. *Maybe this would be a good time to visit it,* she thought. She could be back in a few minutes, certainly before Polly would need her in the kitchen.

The water was colder than she expected, and Alice shivered as it crept up to her knees. It had been a dry spring and the river was low, so it didn't take long to reach the other side. She headed into the woods in the direction from which she had seen the Indians approach the Rushes' ranch.

Toward the middle of the morning, Frances came into the kitchen.

"Polly, when Alice finishes helping you, would you send her upstairs? She can sew while Mama and I cut quilt blocks. I should have told her that this morning."

"Yes, you should have," Polly agreed. "She's already off daydreaming somewhere. She carried all these jars up from the root cellar, and I let her have a little time off before we start hulling berries. She's probably down by the river."

Frances frowned. "Why didn't she come upstairs? She knew her sewing wasn't finished. When is she going to learn to be responsible?"

"How soon we forget," Polly said. "I don't recall you was running around looking for work when you was ten years old. She'll grow out of it, same as you did."

"I suppose I'll have to go and find her," Frances said. "I'll send her down when you're ready for her."

Frances rounded the house and headed for the river. She

had to admit that the day was better for being outdoors than staying in the house. The cottonwood trees still looked fresh and new, and the breeze was just warm enough to be comfortable. It was hard to imagine that in just a few weeks the hot prairie sun would make the house inviting. She glanced toward the old soddy where the family had lived for most of their first year in South Dakota. It was still a retreat during the summer storms and unbearable heat, but the big house was certainly better for everyday living.

At the river, Frances was joined by Will. "It's hot out there in the field," he said. "Luke said to come see if Alice was here, and we could put our feet in the water."

"That's what I came for too," Frances said.

"You're going to wade?"

"No." Frances laughed at the little boy. "I was looking for Alice. It would be fun to stay here, but I don't want to leave Mama working alone. I guess Alice hasn't been with you?"

"Nope. Haven't seen her since breakfast."

"Maybe she's playing in the soddy. Want to have a look?"

Frances and Will stepped into the little underground house and looked around. The interior was dim, and it took a few minutes for their eyes to adjust.

"Remember when we lived in here?" Frances asked.

Will nodded. "I was just a little boy then. I slept over there." He ran to the bunk bed built against one of the walls and sat down. "You and Alice slept over there."

"Right. And the organ was in this corner." It hadn't been easy, Frances recalled, to convince Papa that the organ had to be moved from Willow Creek with them. But he had relented, and everyone admitted that the instrument had relieved many hours of loneliness.

Frances was proud of the way Simon was learning to play.

"If we lived in town," she had told Mama, "I could give music lessons for a living. But no one wants to come this far out on the prairie to learn."

Will was ready to leave. "She's not here, so she has to be back at the house. Let's go see."

Frances agreed, and they returned to the kitchen to see if Alice had been found.

Alice was getting tired. There was still nothing in sight but trees. She wished she had put on her shoes before she started out, but she'd had no idea that the village was this far away from the river. Their friend Silver Wing walked to their place often with her little boy and a new papoose on her back. She never seemed worn out when she got there.

Alice sat down to ponder the situation. She surely must be near the village. It didn't make sense to turn around and go back without visiting someone. Besides, she admitted to herself, the woods looked just as dense behind her as it did in front. If she were on a path, it was hard to tell where it went. As she gazed back and forth, she had to admit that she wasn't sure which way led home, if she did want to retrace her steps.

Well, there's no point in just sitting here, she thought. In a few minutes she would come to a clearing, and someone would be able to show her the way back to the river. The woods were quiet, and only a bird flying from branch to branch or a small animal scampering through the leaves made any noise.

Alice couldn't see the sun, so she had no idea how late it might be. For the first time she began to worry about what Polly would say when she called and Alice didn't answer. There were a lot of berries to get ready for canning, and Polly would be cross if Alice wasn't there to help her. Perhaps she should turn around and hurry back. Uncertain of which way to go, she hesitated. Suddenly a loud crash startled her, followed by the sound of something heavy approaching.

Her heart beating wildly, Alice began to run in a direction she judged to be away from whatever or whoever was coming toward her.

Luke and Simon hadn't finished washing for dinner when Polly's voice reached them from the kitchen. "Don't suppose you've seen Alice this morning?"

"Nope. We got another missing young 'un to look for? When did you see her last?" Luke said.

Polly came out to the porch, wiping her hands on her apron.

"Little after eight o'clock, I guess. Didn't know she wasn't around until Frances came looking for her mid-morning. Frances and Will have already searched everywhere they can think of, but there's a lot of places to be on a couple thousand acres. Alice has never gone off like this before. I can't think what got into her."

Luke wiped his hands and face and headed for the table.

"My guess is she's gone across the river."

Polly shook her head. "She knows she's not to go in the river without someone there, even to wade."

Luke raised his eyebrows. "The only reason for a kid knowing anything is so's they'll have something to forget. A warm morning, cool water, and a woods you ain't explored yet is hard to pass up. Especially if no one is watching and hollering you back."

Simon was stuffing in his dinner as quickly as he could. "I'll go find her," he said.

"Me, too," Will echoed.

"And we lose two more of you? Not very likely." Polly eyed them sternly. "I want both of you having lessons with Frances this afternoon or right here under my eye. You can hull berries and draw water to wash 'em. Luke will take care of Alice."

Neither possibility sounded inviting, but the boys knew better than to argue with Polly.

Manda came into the kitchen with a worried look on her face. "I wish someone could tell me why a child disappears whenever Chad is away from home. Frances couldn't even eat. She's back out there looking every place she went this morning. Where in the world could Alice have gone?"

"We know she didn't go with Chad the way the last one did." Polly looked at Simon, and he ducked his head in embarrassment. He had not been allowed to forget how he had hidden in the wagon when Chad and Henry made their first trip from Willow Creek to the new homestead. Luke had been obliged to ride to the first night's campsite to bring him back. Simon had been only five years old then, but he still remembered the uproar he had caused.

"I'll start up by the reservation," Luke said. "I got an idea she's visiting the neighbors."

"The reservation! She doesn't even know where it is! She couldn't walk that far, could she?"

"We'll find out." Luke gulped the last of his coffee and stood up. "Better wrap me up a sandwich and some cookies. She's going to be hungry. I reckon she'd head straight into the woods and not travel too fast. Might overtake her when she stops to rest. Even with a head start, I think I can catch her before dark. If she gets to the village, she's safe."

"Let's pray before you leave," Manda said. They all bowed their heads.

Luke waited respectfully, but privately he thought that the time would be better spent searching. He wasn't against religion or practices of Bible reading and prayer, but he felt that the Almighty probably expected him to use his wits and get along in life without bothering Him with every little thing that came along. This was especially true when Luke had a pretty fair idea about what needed to be done, as he did now.

Tucking Alice's lunch in one big pocket and her shoes in the other, he set off toward the river. The family trailed behind him anxiously.

"We're going in the right direction," Luke said. "Looks to me like some little girl has been here, and we don't have that many girls around. Don't you reckon she laid out this doll house?"

Manda agreed that it looked that way, and tears came to her eyes. "She'll be frightened if she can't get back home. What will we do if you don't find her?"

"Don't worry. We'll be home before dark. Chances are she's already at the village, and someone will start this way with her." Luke crossed the river and swiftly disappeared into the woods. Slowly the three women and two boys returned to the house. Polly had more help with her jam than she expected, since everyone wanted to stay together until they knew that Alice was safe. It was a long afternoon.

Luke knew that it was at least an hour's walk to the village at the quickest pace, but he really didn't expect to go all the way. He was sure that he would see Alice coming toward him soon. He strode through the woods, enjoying the cool dimness provided by the trees. This was taking time from his work, which had to be carried out alone until the others returned from Nebraska, but Luke had to admit that it was restful back there.

His mind wandered to a poem that Frances had read to the family one evening. He thought it might have been called "Trees." He did recall that it said that only God could make a tree. He looked at the branches towering over his head. Would someone as powerful as that really have time to solve the small problems of people on earth, as Henry and the family believed? If so, should he try to make a bargain with God to help find Alice? Once again, as when Simon had been missing, Luke wished that he knew a little more about praying. He would have liked to believe that he was entitled to ask the Almighty for aid.

Suddenly Luke realized that he was entering the clearing that surrounded the village, and he had not yet seen Alice. For the first time he felt a stab of worry. He couldn't have missed her if she had been on the trail, and she surely wouldn't have left it. He hurried toward the tepee where their friend Silver Wing and her husband Black Wolf lived. Silver Wing greeted him cordially, but with surprise.

"How good to see you. Do you bring good news from my friends?"

"Everyone is well," Luke replied. "I've come to take Alice home. Her mother is concerned about her."

Silver Wing's smile faded, and she looked alarmed. "Alice? But she is not here."

Silver Wing clapped sharply, and when a small boy appeared, she gave him quick directions in her language.

"The men will fan out through the woods," she told Luke. "They'll find her soon. I will return with you."

As they hurried back toward home, Silver Wing explained why Black Wolf was not with them.

"He has gone this week to the mission school to help repair some buildings. We're grateful for the education we received there—and for the teaching about God."

"Don't you have a god of your own?" Luke asked. "I thought the Indians believed nature is their god."

"There is only one God," Silver Wing answered simply. "He is the creator of nature. We do not worship the things He has made, as wonderful as they are."

"I don't think all Indians believe that way," Luke said.

"I've met some who say they don't want any part of the white man's God."

"That is true. And Indians meet many white men who feel the same way." Silver Wing glanced at Luke, but he didn't reply, so she continued. "I've also seen that when they meet trouble, God is the first one they call on."

For a while they walked in silence, and Luke thought over her words. She couldn't know that he had considered doing just that. He had reached the end of what he could do by himself.

"How long will it take your men to start searching?" he asked finally.

Silver Wing looked at him in surprise. "They are all around us right now. Haven't you seen them?"

Luke admitted he hadn't, nor had he heard any noise among the trees.

Silver Wing shook her head. "You won't hear them, but once in a while you will catch sight of one if you look carefully."

As closely as he watched, Luke saw only slight movements in the woods that might have been the wind or running creatures. The closer they came to the river, the more concerned he was that Alice had been carried off and wouldn't be found. He dreaded facing Manda and the others with the news that she was gone.

Running in her bare feet wasn't the best way to travel, Alice found. There seemed to be more slippery pine needles and leaves, as well as tree roots, than she had noticed before. This wasn't the path she'd come on, but she didn't dare turn around to search for it. Whatever was chasing her was falling behind; she could no longer hear the crunch of branches. But what if it had gone around the trees and was waiting to pounce on her? She mustn't stop until she reached the river and could see the house.

All at once Alice was pulled back sharply. Her heart almost stopped when she looked around to see what had grabbed her, then she sobbed with relief. Her skirt was caught on the branches of a fallen tree. The only sound she could hear was her own gasping breath, and as she looked around cautiously, she could see nothing but trees in every direction. Carefully Alice loosened her skirt from the branch. She was glad to see that it wasn't torn. Manda would not have been happy about that, and Frances would probably set her the task of mending it. Gratefully she sat down and leaned against the tree. She would rest for a few minutes, then make up her mind which way home might be. Wearily Alice's head rested on the tree trunk, and she slept.

When she awoke, the woods seemed a little darker than before. How long had she slept? She must make herself get up, or it would be past dinner time at home. She was hungry and thirsty, and there didn't appear to be anything to eat or drink out there. Before she could move, Alice's heart thumped again. A voice shouted something she didn't understand, and the sound echoed throughout the woods until it seemed that there must be a hundred people saying the same thing. At the same time, Alice was lifted from the

ground by strong brown arms and was carried swiftly
through the trees.

The shout reached Silver Wing and Luke, and Silver
Wing smiled with satisfaction.

"They've found her. She'll be at home before we are."

Luke was startled. "How do you know?"

"They just told us. Didn't you hear them?"

"I heard a noise, but I didn't know what it was."

"A happy noise," Silver Wing said. "It is the signal that
the child is safe. It's the quickest way invented to send a
message. One man will bring her in and the others will
return to the village."

Silver Wing had predicted correctly. When they reached
the river, the whole family was gathered around Alice.
Simon saw them coming, and ran to meet them,

"Alice is here! She's already here! Swift Eagle brought
her, and he's gone. Did you see him? How did you know she
was here so you could come home?"

Simon didn't wait for answers to any of his questions but
raced back to the others. He didn't want to miss any of the
story Alice had to tell.

It was an evening of rejoicing for everyone. Silver Wing
was invited to stay, but after lingering just long enough to
join in thanking God for Alice's safe return, she had to get
back to her family. They would meet again soon, she
promised.

When chores and supper were over, it was a sober
and thoughtful Luke who retired to the bunkhouse alone.

He sat quietly looking at the stars, reliving the events of the day. When Henry returned, Luke intended to have a long talk with him about the God who had answered in response to the call of His children.

Plans for
the Future

Chad, Henry, and Ethan returned from Willow Creek the week after the big sale. The family was happy to have them home, and eager to share the news of all that had happened while they were gone. When Alice's story was repeated, Ethan regarded her sternly.

"I thought you were old enough that I wouldn't have to keep my eye on you every minute. Ma told me to look after you, but I can't watch you for the rest of my life."

"I'm sorry, Ethan. I won't do it again."

"She won't have time to," Simon put in. "Frances has her sewing every minute that Polly doesn't have a job for her."

"We don't need your comments, Simon," Chad told him. "I recall your once doing something just as foolish."

Simon grinned, but his face turned red.

Manda was anxious to hear about her friends in Willow Creek.

"Lydia sent you some things. Said she wished you had come along to visit," Chad said. "The schoolteacher asked how Frances was doing with the children's lessons, and all the ladies showed up with good food the day of the sale."

"Did you sell everything, Papa?" Frances asked.

"We did. A lot of things went to the folks that bought the house. Family named Ferguson. Strangers to me, but your Uncle George knew them. It was a successful trip."

In the kitchen, Henry leaned back in his chair with a look of satisfaction. "I'm glad to be home. I missed your cooking, Polly. George's wife, Myra, tries, but she doesn't have the years behind her you have."

"You gave that compliment with one hand and took it back with the other," Luke told him.

"Now, I didn't mean—"

"I'll take a compliment any way I can get it," Polly said. "Cookin' is one thing I'm good at, and I'm glad to have a family that enjoys it. How'd you like the train ride?"

"Have to say it was a mite bit easier traveling than the first trip I made out here," Henry admitted. "Didn't run into any rattlers and didn't get my own meals. Don't know as I'd want to spend two weeks living in a train car, though."

"I'm glad to have you all back," Luke told him. "Simon was a big help, for an eight year old, but he doesn't take the place of a man. Has Ethan said any more about going to school?"

"Nope. He spent some time out on the Boncoeur place with Bert, but he never mentioned school."

"Just as well," Luke said. "He'll have his own place to run when he gets older. The experience will do him more good than book learning."

July was extremely hot and dry.

"I declare, even the springhouse feels like an oven," Polly said. She pushed her wet hair back from her face and fanned herself with her apron. "That wind could peel the skin right off your arms. Don't know what we'd do without the summer kitchen. Scarce any point in building a fire out there, though. The bread'll bake on top of the stove."

Henry and Luke splashed water over their heads when they came in for supper. "There wasn't any cool place to work out there today," Luke said. "Thought for a while I might not make it."

"If you hadn't sent Alice and Simon out with lemonade, neither one of us would have made it," Henry said. "I can't remember the last three summers being this hot."

"They never been any different out here," Polly told him. "You can see the heat popping up off the ground. I'm afraid everything is going to shrivel up and die, including us."

The men sat down to eat the cold supper Polly had prepared. Ham slices, potato salad, baked beans, pickles, fresh bread, and tomatoes would ordinarily be a welcome summer meal. Tonight, however, Luke just pushed the food around his plate.

"Too hot to eat," he said when Polly mentioned it to him. "Guess I'll go out to the bunkhouse and shuck these clothes."

Henry and Polly watched him leave with concern on their faces. "Ain't nothin' ever separated Luke from his meal before he was done with it, even if he had to take it with him," Polly said.

"I'll try to get him to go down to the river and cool off," Henry said. "It was pretty hot out there today."

The next morning, Henry entered the kitchen alone. "Luke says he's going to rest a few minutes more, then he'll be in. But I dunno. He doesn't look good to me."

Polly dropped her spoon and looked at Henry in alarm. "Rest a minute? Luke? He's too stubborn to lie down if he was near dead. He must be sick." She placed Henry's breakfast before him, then headed for the bunkhouse. Ethan was coming from the barn.

"Luke didn't help with the milking this morning?"

"No," Ethan replied. "We told him we would do it. He tried to get up, but I don't think he feels too good. I was going to see if he was coming to breakfast."

Polly was becoming more worried by the minute. "You go on in and eat. I'll see to Luke."

At the door she called to him. The answer was weak but determined. "I'm coming, Polly. Don't get yourself in a knot." There was silence for a moment, then, "Well, mebbe I'm not. Think I'll stay here a bit. You go on back to your kitchen. I'll be fine."

"I'll not be going back until I see what's ailing you, Luke Hawley." Polly stomped in and stood at the foot of Luke's bunk. "Why, you're in the same clothes you had on last night!" She proceeded to strip the shirt from his back, and

Luke hadn't enough strength to resist. "Now, where's your nightshirt?"

At this, Luke showed more life. "I'm not putting on no nightshirt in the morning! And if I did, there ain't no woman going to help me with it!"

The energy needed to make that declaration was more than Luke had to spare. His head dropped back on the bed and his eyes closed. Polly found the garment in question, and Luke was soon lying in a straightened bed with a cold, wet cloth on his forehead.

"If you expect to live out your natural days, you're going to have to let a woman take care of a few things," Polly said. "Now don't you move from there. I'm sending Henry for the doctor. You're a sick man."

When young Dr. Flynn arrived, he agreed with Polly. "Breakbone fever," he said. "It'll take a while to get over it. He'll need good nursing."

"I can't spend my days running between here and the house," Polly said. "Is this stuff likely to go through the family?"

The doctor shook his head. "No. It's the result of an insect bite. If you keep mosquito netting around his bed, it likely won't spread to the others."

Chad and Henry were able to get Luke to the house. Manda set up a bed in the parlor, and the room was forbidden to the children.

"Should be out there working," Luke muttered weakly when Polly brought soup to him.

"You ain't needed out there to watch the wheat grow,"

Polly told him. "You'll be needed to harvest it, so lie still and get well."

"Ain't never been this sick before. Feels like my legs is going to drop off, and my back is broke. How long's this stuff supposed to last?"

"Quite a while, the doctor says. But he never knowed anybody to die from it."

"Don't know whether that's good news or not," Luke groaned. "Seems like it might be better to get out of my misery."

Henry came to visit him in the evening. "We sprayed the bunkhouse and put screens on the windows," he said. "Too bad we didn't think about doing it before you got sick."

"Do you think the Lord is punishing me for saying I'd take my chances on living long enough to get right with Him?"

"Nope. That's not the way He works. He's merciful, and He's giving you more time to straighten things out. Won't hurt none to think it over while you can't do anything else."

Luke had determined to do just that, but it was hard to keep his mind on anything when the fever rose and every bone in his body seemed to ache. Manda and Polly kept him supplied with cold drinks and ice chips, as well as cool cloths for his head. The days all seemed the same as one week passed, and then two. When he finally tried to sit up in the bed, Luke discovered that he had no strength to do so.

"I'm worse than Alice's rag doll," he complained. "The fever sure did take the tuck out of me."

While the women looked after Luke, four other members of the family worked quietly on plans for their own futures.

Henry and Ethan took care of the chores and the field work, along with Chad, who rode out to check on his sheep and cattle that grazed on the prairie. In the evenings, Chad seemed preoccupied with his account books and papers, and seldom entered into family conversations or activities.

Ethan's visit with Bert had increased his determination to attend school in the fall. When it became clear that Luke was indeed getting better, Ethan carefully penned a letter to his friend.

July 15, 1911

> *Dear Bert,*
>
>   *Luke has been very sick, so I haven't told Chad that I plan to leave as soon as the crops are in. I will ask him for the money I've earned and come as soon as I can, probably by the end of September. I'll stay until April, time for spring planting.*
>
>   *Ethan*

The problem of how the letter would be mailed was solved for him the following day at dinner time.

"I need some things from town," Manda said. "We also have to get more medicine from the doctor's office for Luke. I can't take the time to go in and leave Polly with everything to do."

"I'll go, Mama," Frances said. "Alice can keep me company. It won't take long in the new buggy."

She didn't add that she had business of her own in town, and had been waiting for an opportunity to go without having to answer questions about her errands.

As soon as dinner was over, Ethan followed Frances to the springhouse. "Frances, will you take my letter to town? I'd like it to get to Bert right away."

Frances nodded, and the following morning she tucked Ethan's letter into her bag, and she and Alice were on the way before the sun had climbed far above the horizon.

She listened to Alice's chatter and answered her when she asked a question, but Frances had her mind on other important matters. She intended to visit Elaine Flynn, the doctor's wife. Mrs. Flynn had been friendly to her, and Frances felt that she could confide in the older woman.

Leaving Alice to look in the shop windows and play on the town green, Frances promised to return for her within the hour, and turned her steps toward the doctor's home.

"I would like to teach school here in Winner this fall," Frances said. "Do you think there's a chance that I could get the job?"

"They're talking with several people about taking the school," Mrs. Flynn told her. "I suggest that you put your name on the list, and the school board will interview you."

She smiled at Frances and patted her hand. "I'm sure you would make a wonderful teacher. Does your father approve of your applying for the school?"

"I haven't talked with him about it yet," Frances

admitted. "Everyone has been so worried over Luke that there hasn't been time. But if you think there may be a chance, I'll do it right away."

All the way home Frances rehearsed what she would say to Papa. After all, she was going on nineteen and had proven herself a responsible young lady. Actually, she thought, there might be more trouble persuading Mama that she was ready to leave home. Manda depended upon Frances to help with the younger children. While she didn't object to that responsibility, Frances felt that she was old enough to be out on her own. At least she wanted to try it.

Of all the plans being worked out secretly, Henry's was perhaps the most surprising. The weeks that Luke had been ill were the hardest for him. It wasn't only that he had extra work to do, but Henry was concerned about his friend. When it seemed there was a possibility that Luke might not survive the terrible fever, Henry prayed daily that the Lord would spare him and turn his life around. Luke was a good man, but he didn't profess faith in Christ, and this was a source of worry for Henry. When, during the past week, Luke had asked forgiveness and said that he would dedicate the remainder of his life to the Lord, Henry was happy and relieved. He visited with the older man each evening after supper and encouraged him to pray and read the Bible.

But with so much extra activity at the house, Polly wasn't as observant as usual. No one would have imagined that anything could go on in Henry's life that Polly was unaware of. But one evening Henry went in to talk with Luke while Ethan finished his pie.

"Where does Henry go every night?" Ethan asked.

"He's right there in the parlor with Luke," Polly replied. "I wouldn't call that going anywhere."

"He doesn't stay in there until midnight."

Polly eyed the boy sharply. "Henry don't go anyplace until midnight except to bed."

Ethan shook his head. "He hasn't been coming to bed early. I've seen him take Winnie and ride out toward town."

"You mean he goes someplace on the horse in the evenings?"

"Yep."

"And he never says where he's been?"

"Nope."

"Well, what do you know! Henry ain't ever been underhanded, so he's not sneaking away. I been too busy to notice what's goin' on. I reckon Henry's got him a girl somewhere between here and town."

"A girl? You mean like Amelia over at the Porters'?"

Polly slapped her hand down on the table. "That's the one! Now that you mention it, I've seen him casting looks toward her at church. Did he sit with her at the last picnic?"

"Yep, he did. There were other folks around, but they ate together."

"This is the first time I ever been the last to know when something like this was going on," Polly mourned. "Looking after Luke has kept me too close to the house. What do you know about that!"

Polly lost no time approaching Henry on the subject.

Yes, he admitted, he'd been seeing Amelia for some time. She was a right nice young lady, and he was planning to ask her to marry him.

"I'm thinking of arranging with Chad to build a little cabin on my section," Henry told her. "I don't want to go off and leave him. He's been good to let Luke and me each get our own land and graze our own stock with his when we're ready. Seems like a good time for me to do that."

As it turned out, Henry's plan was the only one that had a chance of working out as anyone had envisioned. In the middle of August, Chad announced that the family would leave again to stake a claim for more land. This time the homestead was in Mexico.

Plans
Postponed

The evening sounds of the prairie whirled around the group gathered on the porch of the big house. Luke had been brought out to enjoy the slightly cooler air of the early twilight. The others were gathered about, grateful for the approach of night after an oppressive day in the field and the house.

Now everyone stared at Chad in disbelief. He didn't look at any of them, but continued to study the piece of wood he was whittling.

Finally Will broke the silence. "Where's *Mexico*?"

"Not in this world," Polly declared. "If you have to take on more land, why couldn't it be somewheres nearby, like Minnesota or North Dakota, or even Wyoming, where George is going?"

"Papa! Why *now*?" Frances wailed.

"How long have you been thinking on this?" Manda's

voice was resigned. "Seems to me we've been picked up and moved enough for this lifetime."

"This may be our biggest chance for this lifetime," Chad answered. "I've been hearing of it for some months, and the trip to Willow Creek settled my mind. Just wait until I tell you all about it before you start moaning."

"Are we all going, Papa?" Simon sounded anxious.

Ethan understood how he felt. He recalled the day back in Willow Creek when Chad had announced he was filing a claim in South Dakota. Ethan hadn't known whether all the Coopers would be included; were he and his sister and brothers really a part of the family? It took a long time to be absolutely sure that one was accepted after being hustled around from one place to another so many times.

"Yes," Chad answered, "everyone but Henry."

Manda gasped. "Not Henry? Why ever not?"

"I'll let him tell you about that."

Henry grinned and blushed. "Well, it seems like the Lord might have worked things out just right. I'm wanting to get married as soon as I can, and when I asked Chad about putting up a cabin or staying in the soddy until I could build us a place on my section, he offered to let us stay in the house until you come back."

"You can't run this place by yourself," Polly said. "I know the range animals don't take daily care, but the barn stock is more than you can handle alone. Not to mention my garden and the wheat and corn."

"Won't do it by myself," Henry said. "Amelia's brothers will come to hold the bunkhouse down. We can hire day help when we need it. Amelia's a good cook, too. Of course not as good as you, Polly," he hastened to add, "but we won't starve."

Polly settled back in her chair and glanced at Luke. "What are you grinning about, Luke Hawley? I guess this suits you just fine, don't it? You've had an itchy foot ever since you scared your ma to death walking into town when you was only three years old."

"Yep, I'm real pleased. I've always wanted to see a foreign land."

Will had been listening to all the conversation, but now he became impatient. "Well, where *is* Mexico?"

"It's four states directly south of us," Frances told him. "Farther than you've ever been before. When are we going, Papa?"

"Soon as the wheat and hay are in. Several families from Willow Creek are making up a caravan to go together. They'll be glad to have a teacher for their children, I've no doubt."

"I hope they're prepared to pay me," Frances said. "I could possibly have a school in Winner if I were going to be here."

Chad looked at her in surprise. "I guess you're right. They should pay a little for regular lessons. We'll talk it over."

Ethan had said nothing. He sat on the steps and stared off across the prairie. Why should his plans for school be abandoned? He would be fourteen years old in November, and he did as much work as any man on the place. Chad

had said he could make his own decision. When it was time to leave, he would simply tell the family that *he* was going to Kansas.

Somehow the thought didn't make him as happy as it should have. Somewhere in his mind he could hear Ma saying, "Take care of the little ones, Ethan. I'm trusting you to be responsible." And another voice, that of Matron Daly at Briarlane Home, also echoed in his mind. "The Lord will lead you where you should go if you trust Him."

Ethan looked at Alice and Will and Simon. What dangers might they meet in a strange place, and not have him to turn to? Would a year of school be worth it if anything happened to one of them, and he wasn't there?

With a sigh, Ethan decided that it would not. If they were going to be here, in a familiar place, he might not worry. But in another country? Ethan wouldn't even be able to picture where they'd be; he didn't know anything about Mexico. He turned his attention to what Chad was saying.

"Mexico has a new president, and the United States is putting a lot of money into the country. Some big oil companies are going down there, and work will be plentiful. I figure that if I get some land now when things are beginning to prosper, I'll be able to sell it later at a profit. Mexico has a system of land laws that allows United States citizens to do that. In fact, they're encouraging it."

"Chad ain't never needed no encouragement to get him more land," Polly grumbled as she took a cold drink to Luke at bedtime. "He didn't say a thing about what we'll live in when we get there."

"Probably a 'dobe house," Luke said.

"What in the world is that?"

"Mud." Luke grinned at Polly's shocked expression. "You can be glad it's on top of the ground. It won't be a soddy."

"My, my. Aren't we fortunate. I was just getting used to having a hardwood floor to scrub again. Now I can go back to one that won't show the dirt. I suppose everyone will be in the same room, too. We don't know a soul that's ever seen that country. How do we know what we'll find there?"

"I can think of a few things," Luke told her. "It's like a desert, so there will be cactus and rocks and plenty of heat. We'll also have another language."

Polly sat down in the nearest chair and stared at Luke. "Another language? You mean those folks don't speak no English?"

"Nope."

"What, then?"

"Spanish. I met some cowboys once that could say a few words. They said you learn to talk to the people when you've been there awhile."

Polly shook her head. "I'm feelin' better all the time. If it wasn't for helping Manda with them young 'uns, I'd stay right here."

"You wouldn't want to miss all the excitement," Luke said. "How many ladies your age get to leave the United States? Chad says we'll live in a town and not way out in the country. You can visit with the neighbors."

Polly glared at him. "Sure I can. We can talk about two different things at the same time and never know the difference. I'm going to bed. Chances are I won't sleep a wink for counting my blessings."

The heat continued without a break, but the work went on as usual. Fresh vegetables and fruit were canned to replenish the root cellar, and almost everyone took part in the job. The men and Ethan gathered a fresh supply each morning while the ground was still wet with dew. Simon and Will were set to stringing beans, shelling peas, cutting tops from beets and carrots, and stripping the outer leaves from the cabbages. Frances and Alice washed, cut up, and peeled bushels of everything, while Polly and Manda supervised the cooking and canning. It was a never-ending job.

"We ain't even started the butchering yet," Polly said. She wiped her face with a wet towel and sat down at the table for a minute. "We got a lot of meat to put down."

Manda nodded. "I'm thinking we'll make a quantity of jerky to take on the trip. It's a long way, and ice won't keep more than a few days."

"That'll do for getting there, but it won't hold us all winter and however much longer we stay."

"I'm not worrying about that. I told Chad that I wasn't planning to lug a year's worth of food across the country. We'll live like the people there live and eat what they eat."

"Hmph." Polly was skeptical. "And what might that be?"

"I don't rightly know, but just about everyone in the world eats bread and meat and vegetables. I dare say we'll find something that looks familiar."

"Probably a whole lot that ain't, too," Polly sniffed. "I'm gettin' past the age of making a good pioneer."

The family was glad when Saturday evening arrived and they could turn their attention to getting ready for church. Baths were dealt with quickly. The men and boys elected to carry soap and towels to the river, thus taking care of six people at one time. It was a cooler group who gathered on the porch to enjoy the end of the day. Simon and Will had energy left to chase fireflies and put them in a jar that Polly provided.

"Do you suppose we can get enough in here to be able to read by?" Simon asked.

"You might have a little trouble getting them all to turn on at the same time," Luke said. "And they won't live long enough without air."

"We better let 'em go, Will," Simon decided. "They look prettier flying around anyway."

"What's that funny noise coming from the trees?" Alice asked.

"Cicadas," Chad answered.

They listened to the high-pitched sound for a minute.

"Are they birds?" Simon asked.

"No, they're insects. They only hatch out every seventeen years. We haven't heard them since we've been here."

"The Bible calls them locusts," Manda said. "God sent a plague of them into Egypt so that Pharaoh would let the children of Israel leave the country."

"Did Pharaoh let them go?"

"He said he would, but he didn't. The locusts didn't stay long, but they ruined the land while they were there."

"I hope the cicadas don't do that to us," Simon said.

"They can be pesky and fly into your face," Luke said, "but they aren't likely to clean us out. I wouldn't worry about it."

Sunday was another hot, clear day. Early morning found the family ready to leave for Winner to spend the day. Picnic baskets were stowed in the wagon, and Luke took the reins to drive to church.

"Feels good to be out and able to go again," Luke declared. "The service will mean a lot more to me than it did before I got sick."

They rode briskly down the road between the fields of corn. "Be shoulder high in a couple of weeks, if this weather keeps up," Chad remarked. He surveyed his crops with pleasure. "I'll miss plowing and planting next spring, but we'll be back in time for harvest."

"The Lord willing," Polly added.

"Yes, the Lord willing," Chad said.

"Aren't we going to have a farm in Mexico, Papa?" Simon asked.

"Not exactly. Remember I told you that we were planning to sell the land? First we will drill for oil. The folks that are going there from the big companies will buy the land if we find oil."

"It won't be as pretty as our fields, will it?" Alice said.

"No, it won't," Manda answered for Chad. "Nothing is as pretty as these green leaves and sprouts of corn." She glanced at Chad. "We'll all miss it."

Chad remained silent for the rest of the trip, and the children wisely said nothing more about Mexico.

The small church was crowded with worshipers, and after the service it seemed that everyone pounded Luke on the back and welcomed his return after so many weeks.

"I hear you folks are joining the caravan to Mexico," the minister said. "That's a pretty long trip. Staying a year, are you?"

"We plan to," Chad replied. "I've filed on several sections, and it will take that long to see whether it's going to be profitable or not."

"Taking a chance, aren't you? What if your claim is a pile of rocks that won't even grow cactus?"

"Don't think it will be," Chad replied. "We have to take the land agent's word for it, but if he tries to hoodwink all of us, he'll be in big trouble."

Dr. Flynn wandered over while the ladies were putting out the dinner. "I happen to know that this is the best food around," he said. "Polly sure got you back on your feet, didn't she, Luke?"

Luke happily agreed that this was so, and Polly looked pleased. "Go along with you, Doctor. You just saw this berry cobbler and thought you'd get a piece of it. Why don't you and the missus join us for dinner?"

"We'd be happy to do that. I think Elaine is already over here talking to Frances."

He sat down with the men, and they were soon discussing the crops and the coming trip.

"You're leaving your place in good hands, Chad," Dr. Flynn said. "Henry and Amelia are capable young people, and her brothers are good workers. We'll miss all of you—especially on Sunday when Frances isn't here to play the organ. You have a wonderful family. Make sure you don't lose any of them in Mexico."

Will had been listening to the conversation; now he wandered over to where Ethan was sitting with some of the older boys. They were talking about Mexico too.

"You're lucky, Ethan. I wish I could travel like that." Sam Goode sighed. "I'll spend the rest of my life on the farm and maybe get to town on the Fourth of July."

"You come in to church every Sunday, Sam."

"I don't count that as going to town. This is the only thing I see." Sam looked around at the woods surrounding the little church on three sides, and then out across the prairie they were facing.

"Hey! Look at the dark clouds coming in! Do you suppose it's going to hail the way it did two years ago?"

The boys stood and watched the black clouds come closer. The men stopped talking and walked to the edge of the churchyard. Very soon the sun was covered, and the bright day had turned to dusk. Mothers gathered their children and headed for the church.

"Hurry and get inside! We're going to have a downpour!"

"Them ain't rain clouds. We'd best take shelter." One of the older settlers turned and headed for the building, and the others followed quickly. As many as could crowded around the windows to watch the ominous blackness approach. There was silence in the church. Even the small children watched wide-eyed while objects like pebbles hit the panes of glass, and the room was darkened.

Simon tugged at Chad's coat. "What is it, Papa?"

"Cicadas. They're migrating."

One by one the men turned from the windows and slumped onto the benches.

"They'll be past us soon," said one. "We can go on home and start over."

"Too late for corn, but mayhap we can get some late wheat," said another.

"We'll share what they didn't get. Sometimes they only cut a swath a mile or so wide."

It was a solemn group that headed for home late that afternoon. As far as they could see on either side of the road, the prairie grass had been stripped to the ground. When they reached the outer boundaries of the farm, their worst fears were realized. The corn and wheat were gone. Not one blade of green nor sheaf of gold remained. It was as if some giant mower had moved through while they were away and flattened everything in its path.

"Where did it all go?" Will asked. "What happened?"

"The grasshoppers ate it," Ethan told him.

"Did God send us a plague like he did Pharaoh?" Alice looked frightened.

"No," Chad said, "they are just doing what is natural for them. When it's been hot and dry for a long time, they migrate from one part of the country to another. They travel in big swarms like those we saw today, and they eat everything in their path."

Henry and Amelia joined the others at home. Polly prepared supper, but her heart wasn't in it. "All the food we saved is what grows underground or we've already canned. Nobody's going to starve, but this is one desolate looking place. Looks worse than it did when we came."

"It will look brand new again by the time you get back here," Henry told her. "This won't happen two years in a row. We'll replant whatever we can right away."

If Chad were discouraged, he didn't show it. Preparations went ahead for their departure, and when they were ready to leave in September, the prairie was beginning to look green and things were returning to normal.

5

SOUTH TO A
NEW LIFE

By the time the group was ready to leave Willow Creek, Nebraska, there were only three families making the journey. One family had decided to leave later, another had illness and abandoned the idea. Two others admitted to being fearful.

"I hear tell that's wild country down there," Ed Swartz told Chad. "I don't want to get into the middle of a civil war."

Ben Archer chimed in. "Yes, and they're having trouble with bandits. Some of the revolutionaries are coming right on over to the United States—crossing the border as if it wasn't even there!"

Chad listened politely, but he wouldn't be turned back by threats of danger. "We'll be as safe there as we are at home in South Dakota. We aren't far from Fort Randall, and they have a regiment there that does nothing but settle the

range wars. Some homesteaders have barb-fenced their land
so's the Indians can't graze their stock or hunt buffalo.
Doesn't make for good feelings, I can tell you."

"Don't think it's a land dispute in Mexico," Ben said.
"Seems more like they're fighting over the government.
And if the United States has their own folks down there,
they're going to want to have a say in what goes on."

Chad nodded. "Could be you're right. But I'll stay out of
their politics. I'm just going to homestead my land, sell it,
and come back."

Manda was disappointed to find that Lydia Archer would
not be going. "I thought we might be neighbors again. I
don't know Emma Sellers or Mary Brook as well."

"You'll have plenty of time to get acquainted," Lydia
predicted. "You'll be in pretty close quarters for a while."

The prospect didn't enchant Polly. "I remember our last
move, and it was only into the next state. I don't look
forward to havin' my home move under me for however
long it takes to get there. And how many young 'uns are we
going to have to look after?"

"The Sellers haven't any small ones," Lydia said. "A
fifteen-year-old boy and a girl seventeen. The Brookses
have two girls, eight and eleven."

They decided to travel by train. "With fewer people than
we expected, it will be cheaper and faster than taking the
wagons," Chad said. "Seventeen people can ride
comfortably in one train car, and it won't take much over
two weeks to reach the border in El Paso."

The morning of their departure from Willow Creek,

Ethan sat on a trunk and leaned against the station house. The familiar smell of the railroad yard tar and gravel dust surrounded him. He had only to close his eyes to bring back the scene of his arrival at this station five years before. He had been about the age Simon was now, and although he hadn't admitted it, even to himself, he'd been afraid. It had been less than a year since Ma had died, and he and the others were just getting used to the Briarlane Christian Children's Home, where Matron Daly had cared for them so lovingly.

In his mind, Ethan saw the big steam engine, puffing and snorting, the long trail of cars behind it, and the two coaches that were the orphans' home. It had taken two weeks, with frequent stops to leave children in towns along the way, to reach Willow Creek. Today he would be leaving on a train again, but not as an orphan. There was another difference, too, that mattered to Ethan even more. He was leaving without his friend Bert. They would not be going to school together this year, and Ethan didn't know how long it would be until he could see Bert again.

Suddenly, as if in answer to a wish, someone poked him on the arm. Ethan looked up at Bert's freckled, grinning face.

"Papa let me ride in this morning to see you off," Bert said. "So you're really going to Mexico?"

"It looks that way. I sure wanted to go to school with you this fall."

"Hey! You can do that next year! Aren't you excited about traveling so far away?"

"Yeah, I guess I am," Ethan admitted. "Maybe you get to go to another country only once in your life."

"Some of us don't get to go that often," Bert said. "You don't know what it'll be like there, but you sure know about living on a train." He thought for a moment. "I guess it's a little like going to a home you don't know anything about, but at least you're used to the people you're with."

Ethan nodded. "I need to keep my eye on the others too. Maybe you ought to come along to see that I don't lose anyone."

"I wasn't much help when you lost Will back at Briarlane. And remember Simon following that itty-bitty circus lady with the hat and purse? Who knows what they'll find to do in Mexico?"

"That's what I'm afraid of," Ethan sighed. "I suppose I'll always be responsible for them."

Bert regarded him soberly. "Listen, Ethan. You got to start living your own life. They've got a papa and mama to look after them now. You won't be watching out for them every minute when you go away to school. You might's well begin getting used to it now." He picked up the bag he had dropped beside him. "I almost forgot. I brought you something to take on your trip."

Bert dug out a book and handed it to Ethan. "Remember this?"

"The drawing book I gave you when we came here!" Ethan looked at his friend with amazement. "You still have that after all this time?"

"Sure. Don't you still have the key I gave you?"

Ethan pulled a big key from his pocket. "Of course. I'd never lose this. It reminds me that God will help me whenever I pray." He turned the key over in his hand. "I'll probably need it lots more too. But, Bert, why are you giving back my book?"

"I want you to use it while you're gone. You can draw pictures to show me where you've been. It's not yours to keep—I want it back with more pictures in it."

Together they spread the book out and looked at the pictures Ethan had drawn five years before. They started with the Briarlane Home where both boys had lived.

"Here's the day we left." Bert pointed out the train and the people gathered around to see them off. "I wonder how Hugh is getting along?"

"He's probably a big banker by now," Ethan said, "or at least working with his father at the courthouse."

Bert nodded. "And look—here's Hull House in Chicago where we waited for the Orphan Train. Are you going through Chicago this time?"

"No. Luke says we'll be going west to Colorado, then south to Texas. We'll go through New Mexico, too."

"I kinda wish I was going with you," Bert said wistfully, "but I don't want to leave my folks. I'll be lonesome just going to school in Kansas."

"Next year, I'll be there too," Ethan assured him. "Chad says we'll be back for harvest."

Bert picked up some pebbles and tossed them across the tracks. "You still don't call him Papa, huh?"

Ethan shrugged. "He didn't seem to want me to when we

came, and I just never got in the habit. But he's been a father to me. I never thought much of my own pa. Chad takes good care of us. And he doesn't lose his temper as much as he did when I was younger. I guess I've learned a lot."

Things were getting too serious for Bert. He jumped up and challenged Ethan. "Come on. I'll race you down to the water tower."

By the time they returned, warm and out of breath, all the passengers were gathered at the front of the station, and the baggage was ready to load. Ed and Rilla Swartz, along with Ben and Lydia Archer and other neighbors, had come to see them off.

Rilla Swartz was in tears. "Probably never see 'em again," she sniffed. "Them bandits will have 'em before the year's out."

"What's bandits going to do with all them folks?" Ed scoffed. "If they was smart enough to catch 'em all, they'd be too smart to keep 'em. Especially Manda Rush and Polly. Now there's two ladies as would have their freedom right quick." Ed chuckled at the thought. "And Chad would have all their land took over. Nope. The bandits won't touch that bunch."

In a flurry of last-minute activity, everyone boarded the train, and all seventeen travelers were ushered into one coach.

"Haven't had a bunch this big going south before," the conductor told them. "Had a big church group from Russia that settled up north a few years back. In fact, the railroad took 'em up free because the folks was staking out land the company wanted to get rid of." He helped the men put bags and boxes on the overhead shelves. "Too bad they don't have that arrangement going south. At least you have a coach that will go clean to the border. That's as far as our rails run. I think you'll be comfortable here. You let me know if you need anything. I'll give you notice when we're coming to a town so's you can get off a bit if you want. Here's blankets and pillows, and the dining car's up ahead. You make yourself at home and I'll see if the baggage car's loaded."

"Chatty, ain't he?" Polly watched the conductor return to the platform, then turned her attention to the car that would be their home for awhile.

"Good thing Ma's not alive to know about me going off the edge of the earth. She never trusted these trains neither. Called 'em 'iron monsters breathin' fire.' I call 'em dust buckets. Time we get where we're going, we'll be so crusted over we won't be cleaned up until we start back."

"I don't think it will be quite that bad," Manda said. "It's not like living in a house, but we can keep some order, even if it is in a small space."

The engine hissed and steamed as it moved slowly away from the station. Ethan stood in the door and watched Bert until Willow Creek was out of sight. Ethan had made friends at church in South Dakota, but somehow none was the same as Bert. He and Bert had shared a life that the others knew nothing about. Being an orphan did make you different from regular folks, Ethan decided.

They had not gone many miles before the travelers had the living arrangements worked out. So that each family could have privacy, extra blankets were hung across the aisle. They could be pulled back during the day to allow visiting and moving about. It wasn't long until the men had devised a set of rules intended to add to their comfort. Five children under the age of ten needed some boundaries.

Luke explained the plan. "One end of the coach is the play area. No running, no ball throwing, no climbing on the seats in the other part of the car. Anyone who forgets can sit beside their folks for fifteen minutes."

The warning seemed to help, because things settled into a regular routine very soon. The younger children played games while the ladies quickly became friends as they discussed the life ahead of them.

"We certainly don't know what to expect," Mary Brooks said. "No one I've talked to has ever been in Mexico. Do you suppose the people will take us in?"

"I'm sure they will," Emma Sellers said. "We'll need to learn how to talk to them."

Manda bit off a piece of embroidery thread. "We had thought to have Frances teach the younger children while we were there, but I believe it would be better to send them to school. They would have to speak the language, and we could learn from them."

The others nodded. "We need to be able to talk to people if we're going to shop and find our way around."

Polly was concerned. "Do you suppose there ain't a soul there that knows English?"

"Oh, I think there will be," Mary replied. "The oil companies have office workers from the United States. And there must be lots of other homesteaders with all that land around. I'm anxious to see where we'll live."

"Don't get your hopes up," Emma Sellers advised her. "It won't be anything fancy."

Mary laughed. "We never did have anything fancy."

"If you been thinkin' that having water pumped into your kitchen and a floor under your feet was nothin' fancy, you'll do fine," Polly told her. "Far's I've heard, we'll be living in an oversized soddy on top of the ground."

Mary looked startled, but she spoke calmly. "I expect I can carry water again. I did it all the time I was growing up. But a floor does seem like a necessity."

"I thought so too, when we lived in the soddy," Manda said. "But I found out that you can make do with very little if you have to. We'll get on all right."

Frances began to keep a journal of the trip.

> *Tuesday*
> *The ladies talk and sew and seldom look out the*
> *windows. Right now Nebraska looks all the*
> *same, but I'm sure the scenery will change. I'm*
> *getting acquainted with Prudence Sellers. She is*
> *a quiet girl.*

"If Mama does send the children to school," Frances said, "I'm going to try to get a job with the oil company. I don't want to sit around all day."

"Oh, do you think I could get a job too?" Prudence looked anxious. "I'm sure my brother Ted will find something to do, and I'd like some money of my own."

"I don't see why you couldn't. We'll go together to see about it as soon as we're settled."

Friday
Simon called everyone to look at the water we were crossing over. Papa says it's the Platte River. We are not very far from the Kansas border. We only cross the northwest corner of the state.

Sunday
Today we woke up to a beautiful sight. In the distance to the west we saw the Rocky Mountains, and they are covered with snow! Papa showed us on the map that the train will go along the border of four states—Kansas, Colorado, Oklahoma, and New Mexico. I'm glad I didn't stay in Winner to teach. I'd hate to have missed this trip.

Wednesday
We are going south now, and we're following the Pecos River. The children race from one side of the coach to the other when the train crosses a bridge.

"Look!" Will shouted. "Sometimes the river is on this side of the train and sometimes it's on the other side!"

"Sometimes it's on *both* sides," Simon pointed out.

"That's bigger than our river," Alice said. "I wouldn't try to wade across that one."

> *Saturday*
> *The conductor says we will be in El Paso,*
> *Texas, tomorrow. That's as far as the railroad*
> *goes. The rest of the trip will be by wagon, and*
> *it will take two days. Papa says there is a small*
> *village about halfway where we can stay*
> *overnight. The closer we come to Mexico, the*
> *more nervous I am. I wish we didn't have to*
> *leave the train.*

"We thought we was bringin' plenty of food to last this trip," Polly said, "but we've bought more every time we stopped. Never knew it took so much to feed nine people, back when we had it coming out of the garden."

"We might as well get used to it," Manda said. "I doubt there will be any garden there. At any rate, we'll soon know. I can't decide which is worse—to imagine what kind of life you'll have, or to get there and live it!"

Polly thought she could decide. "I just hope that livin' it ain't worse than I imagine," she declared.

6

POLLY'S
ADVENTURE

Polly trudged down the road toward the village market.
With a basket over her arm and a shawl over her head, she
looked like the other women headed in the same direction.
She still was not used to calling the long, fringed shawl a
rebozo, although she had to admit that it was a handy piece
of clothing. It kept the sun from beating down on one's
head and, Polly had observed, it was used as a covering for
the mouth and nose when a sharp wind blew gusts of sand
through the air. The Mexican women would also tie the
ends together and use the shawl to carry things.

A burro with two loaded baskets on his back came up
behind her, and Polly stepped off the road to let him and
his owner go by.

"*Buenos días, Señora,*" the man said, and Polly smiled and
nodded. Friendly, these people were, even if she didn't
know what they were saying most of the time. They had

been in the little village of Galeana, Chihuahua, Mexico, for two weeks now, and just thinking about the new things she had seen and heard in that time made Polly's head whirl.

The family had been met on arrival in El Paso by a wagon sent from the land agent's office. The driver, Reymundo, was most helpful in answering their eager questions. He assured Chad that he would remain with him as guide, translator, and friend throughout their stay in Mexico.

"Will there be a house ready for us when we get there?" Manda asked.

"*Sí, Señora.* The land agent has made arrangements for you to move in at once. The house is furnished. My sister Carlotta has cleaned it well. You will be comfortable there."

"We're a pretty big family. I hope it has room for nine people."

There was silence for a moment, then Chad cleared his throat. "Well, Manda, there will only be seven people in the house. Luke and I will go with Reymundo to survey our land and begin drilling for oil."

Manda was outraged. "Chad Rush! Do you mean that you are leaving us alone in a town where we don't know anyone and can't even talk to the people?"

"Now, it's not that bad. I understand that Carlotta speaks English well, and she has offered to help you get settled. I'm sure she'll be there to see that you have everything you need. And you won't be alone. Ethan is capable of looking after things and will take care of you when I'm not there."

Ethan looked pleased at the recommendation, but since Manda seemed less than impressed at that moment, he said nothing. Reymundo paid close attention to his driving and appeared not to be aware that any disagreement was in the air. Manda leaned back and looked over the surrounding desert. The thought of being alone in a strange land with four children in her care was not pleasing. She would have a word with Chad later.

When the wagon entered the small town, the travelers looked around curiously. It was unlike anything they had ever seen before. Dust rose like a cloud as they rolled down the narrow road toward the square. Polly tried in vain to keep the dirt away from her face.

"We won't get rid of all this grit in time to start back," she muttered. "We'll have to scrub up after we get home."

Frances looked about her with interest. "These people look neat and clean. We can do as well as they do."

Will had eyes for one thing only—the burros. "Is that a little horse? It's no higher than our horse Ned's legs!"

"No, it's a donkey, Will. Donkey's don't do the same kind of work as Ned and Jesse do. They carry heavy loads on their backs, though," Luke said.

"I don't see how those spindly little legs hold them up," Frances said. "They're carrying too much."

"They're strong little beasts," Luke replied. "Besides, if they decide they've worked enough, they just stop. Burros have minds of their own." The little burro that walked beside the wagon rolled his eyes toward them, but he didn't move to the edge of the road. He seemed to be saying that he was there first, and if anyone moved, it would be that wagon load of strange people. The man who was leading him smiled and waved at the newcomers.

"I want a hat like that!" Simon declared. "Did you ever see one so big?"

Reymundo guided the wagon around a group of people.

"That is a *sombrero, mi hijo*. You must begin to learn how to speak Spanish."

Simon looked puzzled. "My name is Simon, not *mi hijo*."

Reymundo nodded. "I know. *Mi hijo* means 'my son' in Spanish. And you are a *niño* or a boy. See there? You have learned three words in our language already."

Simon beamed as he repeated the words, then he asked Reymundo, "What is Alice?"

"She is a *niña*. Just the last letter is different. Many names end in an 'o' for a boy and an 'a' for a girl."

"Do you have a sister named Reymunda?"

Reymundo laughed. "No, I have only Carlotta. But you are learning Spanish quickly."

As they neared the village square, many more burros appeared, laden with fruits and vegetables and other things to sell. Most of the little animals had straps over their backs, from which baskets hung to carry the produce. Some of them had big loads of clothing or rugs fastened with ropes. All of them plodded patiently along, brushing flies away with their tails and flicking their ears.

There were a few other wagons on the road. Suddenly, Ethan called out, "Oh, look at that! There's a smart little burro!" He pointed at a wagon piled high with hay. Walking behind it, the small beast loaded with baskets was munching happily on the hay that hung over the back of the wagon. He looked so contented that they all had to laugh.

"I'll draw that in my book for Bert," Ethan decided. "Burros are a lot smarter than they look."

The wagon pulled up in front of a building on the edge of town. Reymundo jumped down and pointed proudly with a wave of his hand.

"*Está es su casa,*" he said. "This is your house."

Polly was speechless. Sun-dried bricks of mud, water, and straw were the materials used for the structure. Through the open door she could see the floor, hard packed and smooth, but undeniably dirt. The windows had no glass in them, but wooden shutters on the outside of the house would serve to keep out cold and rain. The roof was bright red tile.

While Ethan helped the men unload the wagon, and the other children ran through the yard, Polly, Manda, and Frances stepped into the one large room and looked around.

"Well, it is big," Manda said as cheerfully as she could. "I think we can put up curtains to make separate bedrooms."

"I thought bedrooms was supposed to have beds in 'em," Polly said. "Them little sacks on the floor is what we sleep on?"

Reymundo set down the boxes he was bringing from the wagon. "We'll fill them with fresh straw, *Señora*. The cots are folded up in the corner." He quickly unrolled a piece of heavy canvas and set up a low wooden frame.

"What do you know! I ain't slept on a straw tick since I was a child." Then, seeing the concern on Reymundo's face, she added hastily, "I remember how I loved to smell 'em."

The rest of the furniture was easy to identify. There was a large table, chairs, a dresser, and a cupboard. Upon examination the cupboard proved to contain heavy pottery plates, bowls, and cups. A drawer revealed pewter eating utensils with bone handles. These seemed to be all the household goods that had been provided.

Reymundo watched anxiously as Manda and Polly surveyed the house. They hadn't the heart to show him how dismayed they were, so they smiled bravely, and Manda said, "My, my. It certainly is clean!"

Reymundo looked relieved. "*Sí*. Carlotta scrubbed everything for you. She wants you to be happy here."

When he left to help the men finish unpacking the wagon, Polly whispered to Manda, "I knew as soon as I saw this place that there weren't no kitchen in here. Do I go to cooking outdoors again?"

At that moment Frances poked her head in a back window. "Your kitchen is leaning up against the house."

"Does it have a stove?"

"I think so. I guess that's what this is." Together they looked at the adobe structure. It contained a hollowed-out space to make a fire and an iron grate across the top to hold pots and pans. It stood in the middle of the small room, and Polly circled it carefully.

"I don't see no oven door. Where do you put in your bread and pies to bake?" She looked up at the ceiling. "If this ain't just like an Indian tepee! The smoke goes right out the roof. I declare! Did you ever see the like?"

Polly continued to gaze around the room. "At least there's shelves here and some pots to cook in. And they're clean. Now if I knew what I had in the way of food, I'd feei better."

Polly looked around carefully as she neared the market stalls. She was certainly not accustomed to walking this far to get food for the day, but the house where they lived had no garden where she could pick her own vegetables. There was no springhouse nor root cellar either. Polly had never before had so many new things to get used to.

Now she approached a stall where baskets of big, ripe tomatoes were displayed. Pointing at one basket, she said, "*Cuánto?*"

"Five *centavos, Señora.*"

Polly shook her head. "Too much."

"Four."

"I can get them for three *centavos* down here." Polly turned away.

"Three."

Polly nodded and dug into her bag for three coins. As she transferred the tomatoes to her basket, she thought gratefully of Carlotta.

"When you shop," Carlotta had told her, "don't just say 'I'll take that.' You must say *cuánto?* That means how much? The vendor will always tell you more than it's worth, so you must bargain."

This Polly learned to do quickly, and she was soon able to get the best price on everything she bought. She continued down the row of tables, reflecting on the new foods she had already cooked in Mexico with Carlotta's help.

On their first trip to the market, Polly had stopped in front of a table piled high with small cactus plants.

"I've seen enough cactuses along the road without buyin' 'em to plant in the yard. Do they really sell these?"

"Oh, yes," Carlotta said, "but you don't plant them. They are good to eat."

Polly looked at her in disbelief. "You're joshing us, ain't you?"

"Joshing?"

"That means joking or being funny," Manda explained.

"Oh, no," Carlotta said. "It is not a joke. This is called a prickly pear, and you can cook them many ways. I like them fried, but you can stew them like apples."

Polly hadn't yet fixed prickly pears for the family, but she had tried many other new things. Everyone in Mexico, she discovered, ate a flat pancake called a *tortilla* instead of bread. Polly had watched in fascination as Carlotta showed her how to pat the cornmeal dough on the table, then toss the dough back and forth between her hands, slapping it sharply until it was round and thin. When it was warmed in a skillet, it could be rolled up with a filling of meat or cheese or mashed and fried beans. The family soon became fond of this new food. Polly's *tortillas* weren't as round and thin as Carlotta's, but no one minded.

Polly squinted up at the sun and decided that it was time to be getting home. She would be late with dinner unless she hurried. As she turned back, she saw a boy hurrying down a side street.

"Ethan," she muttered to herself. "That boy has no idea what time it is. If I can catch him, he can carry this basket home."

Quickly she crossed the road and entered the little street. A burro was coming toward her, and Polly backed up against a building to let it pass. When she started again, the street was empty.

"Oh, bother. He's already gone around the corner. But he can't be too far ahead of me."

As fast as she could, Polly continued on. The street twisted and turned, and there was still no sign of Ethan. Confused now, Polly was beginning to tire. Removing the shawl from her head, she sank down on a wooden step in front of a deserted-looking building.

There sure ain't much of anybody livin' back here, she thought. *I ain't seen another soul since I passed that donkey.*

Suddenly two large, black boots appeared in front of her. Slowly she raised her head and looked at the man who was in them. Polly's face turned white, and she moved as close as she could to the building. A bandit! Polly knew a bandit when she saw one. The man was dressed in a black shirt and black pants, and had black hair and a mustache. Even the eyes peering down at her were like pieces of coal in his tanned face. Mutely, Polly held out the bag that contained her remaining *centavos*.

"Oh, no, *Señora*. I do not want your money. I stopped to see if you are lost."

Polly slumped down with relief. "Oh, mercy. You scared me. You speak English, so I guess you ain't a bandit after all."

The man threw his head back and laughed. "I wouldn't say that, *Señora*, but I will do you no harm. May I help you find your way home?"

Polly nodded. "Yes, if you would please, Mr. . . .?"

"Villa, *Señora*," he replied. "Pancho Villa."

7

ETHAN PLAYS
THE GAME

A shadow passed over the cloth on which Manda was sewing. She looked up at the window to see that clouds were gathering in the sky, then she glanced at the clock.

"Goodness! It's getting late! Where in the world is Polly?" She spoke to Frances, who was dusting the cupboard.

"She's probably arguing with *Señora* Raza over two *centavos*. You know how she loves to get the best of those ladies."

"But it's past noon. She left right after breakfast. Where is Ethan?"

"Out in back, chopping wood."

Ethan was summoned.

"I think you'd better start toward the market and see if you can find Polly. Just say that you came to help her with her basket. She won't like it if we tell her we thought she was lost. I tried to get her to take Frances with her, but she insisted that she could handle it alone. I'm afraid she's gotten turned around somehow, and saying *cuánto* to everyone she sees isn't going to get her very far."

Frances laughed. "Yes, and when they don't understand what she says, Polly just says it louder. But she is trying to learn. She's probably on the road toward home right now."

"I'd still feel better if Ethan walked with her," Manda insisted.

Ethan started at once for the market square. The road ahead was empty, but he wasn't surprised. Very soon after their arrival in Galeana, the family discovered that the hours following the noon meal were a time for *siesta*. Life seemed to stop during the hottest part of the day; the market stalls closed down as their owners shut their doors and rested in the nearest shade.

Surely Polly wouldn't be shopping now, Ethan thought. He hurried a little faster, not sure where he would look if she weren't on the road.

He had almost reached the square when Polly appeared. She wasn't alone. Ethan slowed down and looked carefully at the big man beside her. Polly didn't appear to be alarmed, even though she was so small that her head didn't come to his shoulder. Ethan could see that the man was listening attentively as Polly talked. He was dressed in black, and his hair and beard gave him the appearance of one who had lived a rough life. The fact that he carried Polly's basket on his arm relieved Ethan's fears a bit, but he continued to walk slowly until the three of them met.

"Manda sent me to carry your basket, Polly," Ethan said.

"Now, she didn't have to do that. This here gentleman offered to help me. His name's *Señor* Villa."

Polly smiled up at the man, and he extended his hand to Ethan.

"*Buenos días, amigo.* You must be Ethan."

Ethan stared at him. "Yes, sir. How did you know?"

"Your good *Señora* Polly told me about you and your sister and brothers. We have much in common, you and I. I, too, was an orphan. It is a hard life, yes?"

Ethan nodded. "But I have a home. I've learned a lot. And I take care of the others just like I promised Ma I would."

"You are a brave young man," Señor Villa said to him. "Go to school as long as you can. Education will help you to live a successful life."

"Next year, when we return to South Dakota, I'll go to school. This year I want to work and help Manda and the others."

The big man looked thoughtful. "You want work? Go to the newspaper office. Boys your age sell papers. How much you make depends on how hard you try." He handed the basket of food to Ethan. "If you were older, I would hire you. You have the kind of heart I admire."

He lifted his hat to Polly. "*Adiós, Señora.* You are in good hands."

They watched him for a moment as he strode back toward town.

"How did you meet him, Polly? Weren't you scared that

he might be a bandit?" Ethan asked.

"That nice man?" Polly sniffed. "He's as fine a gentleman as I've seen." She paused, then admitted, "I was a little anxious at first, but he offered to . . . carry my things." She wasn't going to admit that she had been lost and in need of rescue. Manda would put up a fuss and insist she not make the trip alone again, and Polly enjoyed being on her own in this strange land.

The following morning Ethan presented himself at the newspaper office. The manager leaned over the counter and looked at him.

"You want to sell papers, eh? I haven't any Anglo boys working for me. All my boys Mexican. You think you sell as much as they do?"

"Yes, sir."

"*Sí, Señor,*" the man corrected him.

"*Sí, Señor,*" Ethan repeated. "I can do it."

The man shrugged and pushed a bundle of papers across the counter.

"Three *centavos* each. Bring all the money back and you get paid tonight."

Ethan sold all his papers, and that evening he returned home with five *centavos*, which he gave to Manda.

"I just walked up to everyone I saw and said, *El periódico?* and most of them took one," he told the family as he ate supper. "They don't see many Americans selling things, I guess. Tomorrow I'll do better."

Manda was pleased. "Chad will be proud of you when he

hears that you're earning money." She placed the *centavos* in a jar on the cupboard shelf. "Maybe you'll have this filled by the time the men come back."

In the next few days, Ethan discovered that he could talk with the other newsboys by using the little Spanish he knew and the few English words they were familiar with. He also discovered that they were not happy when he sold more papers than they did.

"I'm not going to quit selling papers because they don't like it," he told Polly. "They could do better if they didn't spend so much time playing games."

"Nobody likes to be bested by a newcomer," Polly said. "They'll get over it when they get used to you. Wouldn't hurt none for you to play a little too."

"They don't ask me to play with them. They stop their game every time I walk by. I don't think they like me much."

Ethan was surprised then, when one of the boys called out to him as he passed by the alley where they sat on the ground.

"Hey, *gringo!*"

Ethan stopped, and when the boy beckoned to him, he walked over to see what they wanted. The boy, whose name was Carlos, had obviously been around a number of *gringos*, for he spoke English well.

"You sold all your papers?"

"Almost."

"How much money you got?"

Ethan felt the coins in his pocket. "Haven't counted it.

Enough to pay for my papers, I guess."

Carlos jerked his head toward another boy. "Miguel here thinks it's too bad you only get a few *centavos* every day for all that work. He says we should help you earn more."

Ethan was suspicious. "How do I do that?"

"Here. Sit down, and we'll show you. First, everyone puts a coin in the circle."

The four boys each tossed a *centavo* into the ring traced in the dirt. They waited for Ethan to do the same.

"I don't have any money of my own," Ethan protested. "We don't get paid until we go back to the office."

"You don't lose the money," Carlos told him. "Toss one in to see how it works. If you don't want to play, we'll give it back to you."

I need to make friends with these fellows, Ethan thought. *I don't need any enemies here.* Reluctantly, he threw a coin into the circle.

Carlos handed him a pair of dice. "Now, call out a number—any number you want."

"Three," Ethan said.

Each of the other boys called a number.

"Now throw the dice. If someone called the number that comes up, he gets all the coins. If nobody has the right number, we all add another *centavo* and call again."

Ethan did as he was told, but no one had the right number. Each boy tossed in another coin, and it was Gilberto's turn to throw the dice. There was still no winner, and a third coin was added to the ring. This time Miguel rolled a six—the number Ethan had called.

"*Olé!*" Carlos shouted. "You got them all!" He gathered up the fifteen *centavos* and handed them to Ethan. "Isn't that more fun than selling papers?"

Ethan agreed that it was, although he had a feeling that something was not right about this game.

"What about the rest of you? You lost some of your paper money. What will the manager say?"

Carlos shrugged. "It's only three *centavos* apiece. We have that much extra. The papers we don't sell we give back to them. When you play with us you just hand in enough for your papers. You get to keep the rest. How about it. Are you in?"

Ethan looked at the pile of coins. "I guess so," he mumbled. "Now I've got to get back to work."

"Sure," Carlos said. "We'll see you later."

When the day ended, Ethan handed in money for all the papers. The other boys, as usual, had papers left over. The manager grumbled as he took them back.

"You should work as hard as the *gringo*," he said. "He sells his papers every day. What do you do with your time?"

Carlos grinned. "He's just better than us, that's all. He works too hard."

Ethan felt uncomfortable and knew that his face was turning red. He put the *centavos* in his pocket and started for home. The twelve coins he had won in the game felt heavy. He needed to think about this new development. Being one of the boys was a good thing. He didn't want to be an outsider. But he knew that he couldn't give the extra money to Manda. She would need to know where it came from, and he felt that she wouldn't approve of the game. Where, he wondered, did the boys get the money to pay for their papers when they lost? Then it occurred to him that he himself now had enough *centavos* to play and win more. That was how they did it. They played only with their winnings, so there was always enough money.

This conclusion made him feel a little less anxious, but Ethan wasn't as happy as usual when he handed the earned coins to Manda and was praised for working hard.

I did work hard and sold all my papers, he told himself as he tried to sleep that night. What harm did it do to get a little extra now and then, as long as he paid attention to his job?

The next day Ethan played the game with the boys and lost four *centavos*. Well, he had eight left. He would be more careful. In the days that followed, Ethan would win a few coins and then lose a few. He continued to faithfully sell his newspapers and take five *centavos* home to Manda each day, but he was never lucky enough to win a large amount in a game again. Then shortly before Christmas, Ethan found out what happened when one of the boys lost so much he couldn't pay for the papers he sold.

The game went five rounds and no one had called the right number. Twenty-five *centavos* were in the ring—a small fortune, it seemed to Ethan. Everyone had to throw in another coin. Ethan had only one left, and his heart pounded as he tossed it in with the others. Again, the number wasn't called.

Ethan sat back on his heels. "I don't have any more money," he said. "I'll have to quit."

"You got your paper money," Carlos said. "Put one in."

"I can't do that! It doesn't belong to me! How will I pay for my papers?"

"Us fellows stick together," Carlos told him. "If you don't win the game, whoever does will pay for you. If you win, you make up what the other guys lose and pay for their papers. Then you keep the rest. Go ahead—throw it in."

It was two games later when Gilberto won all the money. He scooped up thirty-two *centavos* and stuffed them into his pocket. Then, true to his word, he pulled out two and handed them to Ethan. Carlos took a small notebook from his overalls and wrote: Ethan two *centavos*.

"Next time you win, you pay it back and we'll be even," he said. "You'll probably best us all tomorrow."

"But I won't have anything to play with tomorrow," Ethan protested. "I can't use my paper money every day."

"Look," Carlos said. "You got your money to turn in today, haven't you?"

"Yes, but—"

"Well, tomorrow will be the same." Carlos tried to explain patiently. "We give you a *centavo* to start with like you did the first time. Remember? You won enough to pay for your papers and took a bunch home. Just stay with us and you'll win big. You can't lose—we're always behind you."

Even though he didn't want to play any longer, Ethan knew that he had to pay back the money they had loaned him. Somehow, even when he won occasionally, he was never able to have all the *centavos* against his name erased from the book that Carlos carried with him. Ethan was taking longer to get home in the evening, and when he did arrive, he wasn't hungry. He pushed the food around on his plate, and he no longer told the family about all that happened during the day.

"You see?" Polly exclaimed. "I said you was workin' too hard. I told you that you ought to play once in a while."

Ethan opened his mouth to reply, then closed it again. He couldn't tell them that he had already played too much, and it had gotten him into trouble. Wearily, he went to get ready for bed. He would spend another night trying to figure a way out of the mess he was in.

As he passed the cupboard, Ethan looked at the shelf where Manda had put the jar of coins. Today's total against him had been seven *centavos*. The jar was big, Ethan thought, and no one would notice if he took that money out and paid Carlos. After all, he had earned the money himself. It wasn't as though he were stealing it. He pushed away the thought that he was being deceitful, and that he ought never have gotten into this fix in the first place.

Ethan wasn't able to sleep. To begin with, when he had taken off his clothes, the key that Bert had given him fell from his pocket. As he picked it up, he thought how long it had been since he'd remembered to pray. First he'd been so anxious to make extra money that he could think of nothing else. Then he was so worried about the money he owed that he forgot to do anything but figure out how to pay it back. He lay on his cot and stared out the window beside him.

"What shall I do?" he prayed. "If I get this straightened out, I'll never play that game as long as I live. Please help me know what to do."

Finally, when all the family was asleep, Ethan arose quietly and took seven coins from the jar. Tomorrow he would give them to Carlos and tell the boys that he was through playing. He would work harder to sell more papers and bring home more money. He would replace the seven *centavos* even if he had to get extra jobs to earn them. If he kept borrowing money to play the game, he might not get out of debt for the rest of his life!

Ethan left early the next morning. He hoped to pick up his papers before the others arrived so that he wouldn't have to talk to them until *siesta* time. This was the hour when they played the game in the alley. He wasn't early enough to get ahead of Carlos.

"This is your lucky day, *gringo*," Carlos said. "I think you will win all the money today." He grinned and took off toward the inn and his regular customers. Ethan turned the other way toward the market. His mind wasn't on his work, and several people had to ask him for a paper. He dreaded to have noon come, and yet he wanted the problem to end. For some reason, he felt that the boys were not going to like to have the money back without a chance to play for it.

He was right.

"Are you ready?" Carlos and the others were waiting when Ethan finally appeared. Ethan didn't sit down as usual. Instead, he took the coins from his pocket and held them out to Carlos.

"Here. This is the money I owe you. I won't be playing anymore, so you can take my name out of your book."

Carlos looked at the *centavos* and frowned.

"You can't quit now. You're just ready to earn it all back. Don't you want to make more than just paper money every day? You know you don't always lose. You could win real big today."

Ethan shook his head. "I can't do it anymore. If my family found out that I borrowed money, I'd be in real trouble."

The other boys looked puzzled, and Carlos spoke to them in rapid Spanish. They glared at Ethan and shouted at him. He couldn't understand what they said, but he knew that they were angry. Carlos no longer looked friendly, either.

When Ethan realized that the boy wasn't going to take the *centavos*, he threw them in the circle and turned to walk away. A threatening voice followed him out of the alley. "You can't just quit the game. You'll be sorry, *gringo!*"

8

THE POSADAS

Soon after the family's arrival in Galeana, Manda was pleased to find a small, friendly church outside the village beyond where they lived. They began to attend the services at once, and found that the little mission was pastored by a young couple from America.

"We are so pleased to have you," the pastor told them. "You will learn Spanish quickly as you worship with us. Isabel and I feel very much at home here, and I'm sure you will too."

And they had. The church members welcomed the new family warmly, and included them in all their activities. Several times Ethan had asked Carlos and the other boys to join him there on Sunday, but they shook their heads.

"We attend the big church in the village—whenever the priest catches us, that is." Carlos grinned. "He wouldn't like it if we went to the little mission."

Now Ethan was glad that the boys had refused. It was enough to see them daily in the market square and to wonder what would happen to him because he no longer played their game. Ethan avoided the alleys and back streets as much as possible.

December was cold and rainy, and occasionally there was a sprinkling of snow in the air. It was nothing at all like the high drifts they were used to in South Dakota. Alice, Simon, and Will happily sloshed to school in bright yellow ponchos and returned every day with tales of the day's activities and new Spanish words to introduce to the family at home.

One evening during supper, Simon tipped over his glass, and water flowed over the table to the floor.

"¡Caramba!" he shouted.

There was silence around the table as everyone stared at Simon in surprise. Simon looked flustered and bent over his plate.

"I don't know what he said, but it didn't sound like 'Oh, dear!' to me," Polly said.

"What did you say, Simon?" Manda asked.

Ethan answered for him. "It means something like 'confound it.' We hear it a lot on the street."

"That's not something we would say in English," Manda said, "so we won't say it in Spanish, either. Be careful that you know what a word means before you use it."

Alice had a bit of news to share. "It's going to be Christmas pretty soon. We talked about it at school. We have to have a *nacimiento* in our house."

"What's a *nacimiento*?" Frances asked.

"I don't know. But I know you bring in straw and sheep and cows."

"I ain't about to have no sheep or cows in this house, missy," Polly said as she got up to clear the table. "I think we should have let Frances take care of lessons here. She never suggested that we fetch the livestock into the living room."

"Perhaps you misunderstood, Alice," Manda said. "We'll ask Carlotta about it."

Carlotta soon straightened it out.

"*Nacimiento* is a manger scene. Each family makes its own with whatever they have on hand. Cardboard animals are painted or covered with cotton. You can make a manger and crib from little scraps of wood. The *Niño Dios* is a little doll wrapped in swaddling clothes. Even the poorest family can have a *nacimiento* beside the front door."

Ethan began at once to draw the figures for Simon and Alice to cut out and color. Will fashioned a wobbly crib and collected hay to line it. When the scene was finished, everyone was pleased with the result.

"Now our house will look like the others in the village," Alice said. "Maybe they won't call us *gringos* anymore."

"*Gringo* isn't a bad name, Alice," Frances told her. "It just means non-Spanish speaking."

"We speak Spanish," Simon protested. "We know lots of words."

"It takes more than words to make some of these folks

understand," Polly put in. "Some of 'em don't know their own language when they hear it."

"That's because we still talk like *gringos*," Manda laughed.

"The teacher told me *bueno* today," Will boasted. "I counted to ten in Spanish."

"You're all doing well. We'll be ready for Christmas when Papa and Luke come home."

Ethan tried to appear interested in the preparations for the celebration, but his heart wasn't in it. He so wanted Chad to be proud of him, but he knew that if his father found out about the game and the money Ethan had wasted, he would be disappointed and angry. Ethan found it more difficult to leave each morning, not only because the weather was wet and cold, but because he knew the other boys hadn't forgotten the threats they had made against him. So far there had been no actual harm done, although they did their best to annoy him.

One late afternoon as he left the paper office, Carlos followed him. "Hey, *gringo!*"

Ethan turned and looked at him. Carlos didn't sound unfriendly, but there was no smile on his face.

"You getting ready for the Christmas celebration? Did someone tell you what we do every year?"

"My sister and brothers heard at school. They said there was a parade, called a *posadas*, and they would be in it."

Carlos scowled at Ethan. "You tell them that they'd better not be in it if they want to stay healthy. We don't need any more *Cristianos* like you in this village. We don't like people who can't keep a bargain. You and your family stay out of our celebrations."

Carlos turned and ran, leaving Ethan staring open-mouthed at him. He had thought that the boys might try to hurt him, but he never suspected that they would threaten his family. Did he mean it? There was no point in trying to chase Carlos. The village boy knew the old streets and buildings better than he did. Carlos had boasted that he could disappear and not be found by his own mother if he wanted to.

Ethan trudged home with heavy feet and an even heavier heart. What should he do? If he told Alice, Simon, and Will that they couldn't take part in the *posadas*, then the others would have to know why. And if Chad and Luke were home before the nine-day festivities began, there would be no way that Ethan could keep them all from finding out what he had done.

The rain fell steadily, and Ethan was getting wetter by the moment, but he couldn't walk any faster. In fact, he was tempted to turn around, walk the other way, and not stop until he reached Texas. He would give anything to be on the train north and forget that he had ever seen Mexico. His mind whirled as he remembered the children's excitement the evening before as they reported on the coming events.

"The celebration begins nine days before Christmas," Alice told them. "Every night there is a *posadas*. It's like a procession."

"Yes," Simon broke in. "We all gather at the church and act out the story of Joseph and Mary and how they looked for a place in Bethlehem."

"*Posada* means inn," Will informed them. "You remember there was no room for them in the inn?"

Alice took up the story again. "Each night a boy and girl are chosen to be Joseph and Mary. Mary rides on a burro, and Joseph leads it. Then everyone else follows along and carries a candle."

"And sings," Simon added.

"And Simon gets to be Joseph one night because he sings good," Will put in. "He can bang hard on the door too."

Polly looked startled. "You go banging on doors? Whatever for?"

"They're looking for a place to stay," Simon explained patiently. "If I knock on this door, you're supposed to say 'Go away! We don't have any room here!' "

"Oh, my. I couldn't say that to anyone at my door." Manda looked distressed.

"It's just play-acting, Mama," Simon told her. "You say that, then I say, 'I'm Joseph. Take me in. I need a place for Mary to rest.' "

Will jumped up and down with excitement. "Then you open the door and everybody comes in and they have a party and play games and there's lots and lots of food!"

Alice pulled on Manda's sleeve. "And you know what else? There's a *piñata* to break with a stick, only you can't see it!"

"I'm afraid to even ask what that is," Polly said. "How

you going to break something with a stick you can't see?"

"Let me tell them," Simon said. "You're getting it all mixed up. A *piñata* is a big clay jar filled with candies and toys. They hang it from the ceiling and then all the children take turns being blindfolded and trying to hit it with a stick. When it's broken, every one picks up toys and candy to keep."

"I'm tired already, and we ain't even had a *posadas* yet," Polly declared. "That will be something to see, all right."

Ethan was coming closer to home and feeling worse with every step. How could he tell the children that they couldn't take part in the festivities? They wouldn't understand, and neither would the rest of the family. It would probably be better for everyone if he just didn't go home. But what would happen to the others if he weren't there to watch out for them? Well, he wouldn't tell them tonight. There were still five days left until the *posadas*. He would try to find Carlos and make it up to him some way. Right now he was too wet and tired to think about how he could do that.

The next morning Ethan couldn't get out of bed. He could faintly hear Manda and Polly as they talked.

"High fever . . . we'd better get a doctor?"

Ethan had no idea that they were talking about him. He was so tired that his eyes wouldn't stay open. He did know that every time he looked at them, someone spooned broth into his mouth. What was it that he needed to be thinking about? He couldn't remember.

When Ethan awoke and tried to rise up, Frances was sitting beside him.

"Lie down, Ethan," she said. "You're too sick to get up. Mama! He's awake!"

Manda and Polly rushed to his bed, and Polly felt his forehead. "The fever's gone. I'll get him something to eat."

"I need to go to work," Ethan said. "I'll be late."

Manda shook her head. "No work. You've been sick for three days. You aren't strong enough to be up yet."

Three days! Everything came rushing back into Ethan's memory. That meant only two days remained until the *posadas*. Ethan closed his eyes and moaned.

"Don't worry," Manda said. "The manager knows you can't come for your papers. I asked your friend who stopped by to tell him."

Ethan's eyes flew open. "My friend?"

"Yes. Carlos, I think he said his name was. He spoke English very well. I'm sure he's taken care of everything."

Ethan sank down on his pillow and tried hard to keep the tears back. Things were getting worse by the moment. Could the Lord get him out of this trouble?

"I need to be punished," he prayed, "but the little ones don't. Can You keep them safe? How will I stop them from being in the *posadas?*"

When Ethan woke again, the house was quiet and the sky outside his window was dark. It was not raining, though he could hear the drip-drip from the roof. *It must be very late*, he thought, *since no one seems to be awake*.

Suddenly he heard a soft voice calling him.

"Psst! Ethan! It's me—Carlos. Can you hear me?"

Ethan knelt on his cot and looked out the window toward the voice. Someone stepped closer to the house, and Ethan could see that it was indeed Carlos. His heart pounded, and he hung on the window sill tightly.

"I can hear you."

"I thought maybe you were going to die," Carlos whispered. "Are you getting better?"

Ethan nodded. He didn't seem to be able to speak. What was Carlos planning now?

"Remember what I said about your family being in the *posadas?*"

Ethan nodded again.

"Well, forget about that. You played fair and paid back what you borrowed. I've been covering your papers while you're gone. You'll be back in a few days, won't you?"

"Yes, but . . . why?"

Carlos was silent for a moment. "You never told the manager what we were doing with our money. We figured that you were a real *amigo*, even if you are a *gringo*. Go back to sleep now. *Hasta la vista!*"

Carlos disappeared, and Ethan crawled back under the covers. He fell asleep while he was thanking the Lord for helping him.

The nine days of the *posadas* passed happily, and Ethan was able to join the procession on the last few nights. The best evening of all was *Noche Buena*. On that day Chad, Luke, and Reymundo arrived home.

"We will stay until Twelfth Night," Reymundo told them. "Then we must go back. It is not good to leave the land without supervision in these days."

"Twelfth night of what?" Polly wanted to know.

"Twelve nights after Christmas, we celebrate the coming of the wise men to bring gifts to the Christ Child," Reymundo explained.

"And they bring gifts for boys and girls, and put them in their shoes!" Will added.

"You mean that you hang up your stockings tonight and then twelve days after Christmas you get gifts in your shoes? They sure do celebrate in this country. What will they think of next?"

"Firecrackers!" Simon said. "There are firecrackers on Christmas Day. I told the boys at school that we only have those on the Fourth of July, but they said they don't have any Fourth of July here."

"Well, they *have* one," Alice corrected. "They just don't shoot any fireworks that day."

Chad was pleased when Manda showed him the jar of *centavos* that Ethan had earned.

"That was good work, boy. We'll save the money for your school expenses next year. In fact," he said to Manda and Polly, "we may be leaving here before the year is over."

"Haven't you found any oil on the land?" Manda asked.

"Yes, there is lots of oil. We're negotiating with the oil companies to buy soon. The problem is the political trouble here in Mexico."

"We hear a lot of news from people traveling through the

area," Luke said. "Most of it isn't good for the Americans. Seems that a Mexican leader was murdered by one of his generals, and the United States president cut off relations with the country because the general wouldn't allow free elections. People here don't want America interfering in Mexican affairs."

"We've heard many stories," Reymundo said. "We can't be sure what is rumor and what is the truth, but it doesn't sound good. A group of American sailors was arrested, and when Mexican authorities refused to apologize, your president sent troops to Veracruz—that's not far from Mexico City—and many people were killed."

"Why haven't we heard about this?" Manda said. "Are you in danger where you are?"

Chad shook his head. "No, but we are fortunate to have Reymundo working with us. There is distrust of Americans in many places, so we don't comment on anything to do with the government or their leaders."

"Most of the action is taking place a long way south of us," Luke said. "There is one man who has been driven into the northern mountains around here. He's a general who is called a bandit by some leaders, but the people love him. He is safe in the hills, because he knows the territory well. Every one in Chihuahua will help him to hide until the danger is past."

Polly got up and hurried over to the stove to get the coffeepot. "You suppose he might be around here someplace?"

"Might be," Reymundo said. "But if he is, you'll never see

him. He's not out to harm anyone here."

"Oh, my," Manda said. "That makes me uneasy. What if he shows up and we don't know it? Don't you even know his name?"

"Oh, yes," Reymundo said. "His name is Pancho Villa."

¡Fiesta!

In the days following Twelfth Night, life began to settle back into a routine for Ethan and the family. Chad, Luke, and Reymundo returned to the homestead.

Manda was apprehensive about their leaving. "I feel as though we're about to be surrounded by a revolution," she had said. "If there is fighting where you are, how will we know if something happens to you?"

"We will be minding our own business," Chad replied. "America isn't likely to send troops that far south. The revolutionaries they are interested in are north of here. We'll be safe, and so will you."

It appeared that he was right, for the village of Galeana went about its daily affairs, undisturbed by rumors of bandit uprisings along the Texas border.

Polly too was worried, but she dared not mention it to anyone but Ethan.

"I hope our friend Señor Villa stays up there in the mountains. I don't like to hear that they're hunting him down. I can't believe he's against the United States, no matter what anyone else says!"

Ethan heard bits of news as he went about the village with his papers.

"I see that your country has sent troops to Mexico to protect American citizens and property," the manager said to Ethan. "We're not going to hurt any citizens as long as they keep out of our politics. Mexico can take care of its own problems."

"At least the people here in the village are friendly to us," Ethan said to Frances. "If the fighting comes closer to Galeana, they might not want to have Americans around."

Ethan said nothing to the family about the trouble he'd had with Carlos and the other boys before Christmas. He was thankful that there seemed to be peace between them now. The winter was cold and wet, and often Ethan would see the fellows huddled around a fire in an alley, finding what little warmth they could. Sometimes, when the village streets were nearly empty, Ethan joined them. After months of attending church services and working on the streets, he understood most of what was said in Spanish.

"My uncle says that the revolutionaries are fighting on the Texas border," Gilberto reported. "The people in Texas are coming to watch them!"

"I wouldn't get that close," Filipe declared. "There's nothing to keep a bullet from crossing the border!"

"I guess the *Americanos* think that since it's not their war, they won't get shot. And they probably won't. Papa says that Mexico doesn't want war with the United States."

"Then their president shouldn't send troops looking for our general," Antonio said. "They might as well save their time. They'll never find him. He won't let any American *gringo* see him!"

Ethan listened silently. He knew who they were talking about, and he also knew that at least two Americans had seen him. The general would have nothing to fear from him or Polly, but Ethan figured it would be better not to say anything about their meeting.

On a stormy day toward the end of January, Ethan was trudging back toward the newspaper office. The shortest way, he figured, was through a back street lined with old warehouses. It was the same street Polly had taken on the day she thought she was following Ethan.

He stayed close to the buildings, even though they didn't provide much shelter from the pouring rain. With his head down, he collided sharply with someone coming around the corner. The man reached out to steady him.

"Ah, we meet again, *mi amígo*."

Ethan looked up into the face of Pancho Villa. Startled, he looked quickly around the deserted street.

"It is all right. We are alone. Come, let's get out of the rain." Pushing open a rusty door, the man led Ethan into an old storeroom. It was cold and damp, but the rain pounding on the roof wasn't falling on them. Señor Villa removed his dripping *sombrero* and shook the water from the brim. He smiled at Ethan.

"You are doing well in the newspaper business?"

"Yes . . . *Sí, Señor.*"

The big man nodded. "I was sure you would. And your friend, Señora Polly. Is she well?"

"*Sí.* She thinks about you a lot, because we hear the news that you are . . ." Ethan paused, since he couldn't think of a polite way to say "wanted" or "hunted."

Señor Villa's eyes twinkled. "Running from the law?" he suggested.

Ethan looked embarrassed, and the big man laughed.

"Many people think I am a bandit and an outlaw. I am accustomed to being the rabbit chased by the hounds." He sat quietly for a moment, then said, "Remember what I say, *amígo.* If I am killed, it will not be by the hands of the enemy or the Americans, but by my own men—my friends."

Ethan shivered, partly from the cold, but mostly because of what Señor Villa had said. "But aren't you afraid?"

"All men have fear, *amígo.* One must be strong and face what life brings. We are alone in this world."

"God is with us," Ethan said quickly.

"God?"

Ethan nodded. "Polly and I pray every day for your protection. The rest of the family doesn't know that we've met you, or they would, too."

Señor Villa didn't respond for so long that Ethan was sure he must be angry.

Finally the man spoke. "No one has prayed for me since my childhood," he said. "I've not thought of God, because I didn't think it mattered to Him. God's people are good, and I am not."

"God doesn't care about that," Ethan said. "He sent His Son to die for you anyway. He really wants you to think about Him."

"Ah, but one forgets to do that when life is hard."

Ethan quickly dug into his pocket and pulled out the key Bert had given him so long ago. "My best friend gave me this. He said that praying is the key to success, and this key would remind me of that when I need help."

Señor Villa was listening carefully.

"I want you to have it," Ethan concluded. "It will help you to remember that God loves you."

The man turned the key over in his hand and looked at it curiously. "And how about you, *amigo?* How will you remember?"

"I've become used to praying since Bert gave it to me," Ethan told him. "Besides, it's not magic or anything. God will hear you whether you have it or not. But sometimes it's comforting to feel it in your pocket. It can remind you that you have a friend who prays for you too."

Señor Villa stood up. "*Gracias, mi amigo.* It will go with me. If I do not see you again, *via con Díos.* I will not forget you nor your good Señora Polly."

Before Ethan could reply, Pancho Villa had opened the big door and was gone. When Ethan reached the street, it was empty.

Although friends at church assured them that spring

came early to Galeana, it seemed to Manda that winter would never end.

"Our daffodils are coming out at home, even through the snow," she said to Polly. "And the lily of the valley. Do you suppose there will be any flowers on the cactuses here?"

"About the same time a lilac bush sprouts by the front door, I'd say," Polly replied. "There's folks that says the desert has a beauty of its own, but I ain't seen it yet."

"I'm getting homesick too. I imagine Henry and Amelia are getting ready to put in a good garden. I've never harvested a garden I didn't put in myself."

Letters from home revealed that progress was being made on Henry's home.

> *Dear Folks,*
>
> *Just a short letter to let you know that all is well here. It was a hard winter. We were snowed in most of February. The boys drove the range cattle in closer before Christmas, so they're doing good. We'll turn them out again by the end of the month.*
>
> *Swift Eagle and the others helped us get the foundation laid for our house before the snow came. Amelia wanted us to be in sight of your place, so we're about half a mile down the river. We're going to start with one floor and build on later. Amelia wishes you were here to help her choose curtains and paint.*
>
> *We hear news in town that things aren't too*

good down there. Some American sailors were
attacked. Did you hear about that? We pray that
you are safe. Do you see Chad and Luke often?
Tell Ethan to take good care of the family while
his pa is gone.

I guess there's nothing new here. We'll be glad
when you get back.

Yrs. respectfully,
Henry and Amelia

Manda read the letter to the family, and then read it over
several times to herself. She longed to see the cottonwood
trees in new leaf and to work her flowers.

"I know Amelia is taking good care of things," she said to
Polly, "but I sure do miss my home. There's nothing like
planting your own garden and taking care of your own
house."

Polly agreed. "My kitchen is going to look mighty good
to me. I guess I should be grateful that we've had it as nice
as we do, but not hauling water to wash clothes or cooking
in a lean-to will suit me fine."

The family had been settled in Mexico for seven months
when spring finally came. May was a beautiful month with
warm breezes and flowers and an occasional gentle rain.
Much to the delight of the ladies, the cactuses *did* bloom.
Red, orange, pink, and white lined the road into the village,
and Polly walked that way as often as she had the
opportunity.

"If I'd 'a known this, I would have planted those homely old things around the house," she declared. "Who'd have thought them dead-lookin' prickles would put out anything as pretty as that! What else have we missed by not being here last spring?"

Quite a bit, as it turned out. Before daylight on the Fifth of May, a boom like a cannon shot startled everyone from their beds and into the middle of the big room.

Simon and Will dived under the table, while Alice clung to Frances. Manda was pale and trembling.

"It's war! They're fighting right out here! Chad said the revolutionaries would stay north of us. Whatever are we going to do?"

Ethan raced to the front window and peered out into the darkness.

"No, it's not war. It's *Cinco de Mayo!*"

"What's *Cinco de Mayo?*" Polly asked, her voice shaky.

"The Fifth of May."

Polly glared at him. "We know what day it is, Ethan! We want to know what's going on!"

Simon came out from under the table. "Oh, yeah. I remember now. We heard about that in school. It's like our Fourth of July, and everyone celebrates all day."

"They certainly aren't wasting any time," Manda said. "We might as well get dressed before the house comes down around us."

No one had ever experienced a day like the one that followed. Mules pulling wagons loaded with brightly dressed families began passing the house in the dim light of the morning. Groups of people crowded the road, all headed for the village.

"Did you ever see such outfits?" Polly marveled. "Just look at the ruffles on that skirt!"

Manda looked over Polly's shoulder. Beautiful horses, their reins and saddles adorned with shiny silver, pranced and tossed their heads. Their riders were every bit as spectacular.

"Those men are *caballeros*," Simon informed them importantly. "They have the most beautiful horses in all Mexico. That's what our teacher said."

"The men don't look too shabby, either," Polly said. From their big black *sombreros*, from which silver coins dangled, to their shiny, black pointed boots, each rider seemed more magnificent than the next. Their snapping dark eyes and drooping mustaches made for distinguished-looking gentlemen.

"Hurry!" Alice urged them. "We need to get to the square before the parade begins."

"I don't know why you didn't tell us about this sooner," Polly grumbled. "We weren't expecting to be shot out of our beds."

"We did tell you," Will said, "but all you said was 'That's nice.' We didn't know the fireworks would be this loud or start so early. They last all day, too."

"We won't have an ear left on our heads," Polly groaned. But secretly she was delighted with the festivities.

The family joined their neighbors and friends from the church in the walk to the village. Everyone, no matter how poor, had *fiesta* clothing, and streets were a riot of color. By the middle of the morning, Manda and Polly were no longer jumping every time a firecracker exploded. They visited every booth on the square and were treated to delicious foods they hadn't sampled before.

The younger children ran off to be with school friends and to get ready for the parade. The ladies, joined by Carlotta, found a small table outside the *panaderia*, and Ethan brought a tray of sweets and *café con leche*. They enjoyed *bolillos dulce* and *bonuelos* dripping with honey.

"Just wait until we get home and I fix these for the men," Polly said. "They may never want pie again."

"I wouldn't count on it," Manda told her. "They'll never give up their pie. They'll just want these in addition to everything else."

"There will be a *fiesta* where the men are," Carlotta told her. "Everyone stops for *Cinco de Mayo*."

At just that moment a roar sounded from the crowd gathered along the edge of the street. High black stallions came thundering by, ridden by shouting *caballeros* who waved their *sombreros* above their heads.

"The parade is starting!" Ethan shouted. "We're in the right place to see it all!"

They would never forget the show they saw that day in the little village of Galeana. Men and women danced in the streets to the accompaniment of accordions, violins, and guitars. Castanets clicked in rhythm with flying feet and swirling skirts. The men threw *sombreros* on the ground and danced around them. There was a dance with swords that left the crowd gasping. People who traveled the roads daily with mules and wagons full of produce suddenly took on a glamorous appearance. The ladies looked on in awe as the music and dancing continued for the afternoon.

Polly was suitably impressed with all but the gypsy who approached their table. Carlotta told them what she was saying.

"She will read your palm and tell you all about your present, past, and future for ten *centavos*."

"You tell her that I know where I been, I know where I am now, and I got a pretty good idea where I'm goin' when I leave here. And it didn't cost me no ten *centavos* to find out."

Carlotta delivered the message, and the gypsy faded into the crowd.

"The idea!" Polly sputtered. "That's like stealin' folks' money from 'em. Who needs someone to tell you what you already know?"

Walking home following a long evening of fireworks, Manda declared that she would be asleep before she hit the bed.

"This has been the longest day I ever remember. And probably the most fun, too. If they plan to shoot off firecrackers all night, I won't even know it."

LUKE'S
MESSAGE

The town of Ocampo, two hundred miles south of
Galeana, was a bustling place that never seemed to sleep.
Numerous hotels and boarding houses in various stages of
disrepair lay on both sides of the rutted road that divided
the town. A boardwalk kept pedestrians from treading
ankle-deep in dust or mud, depending upon the weather.
This was not a family town, although it seemed to be
teeming with people at all hours.

The reason for the activity lay in the surrounding area—
the oil fields. Where other small towns might look out upon
desert grass and cactus, Ocampo saw endless rows of oil rigs,
pumping relentlessly under the hot sun and through the
night. From the town, one could see small figures ascending
and descending the metal structures in the distance,
looking like angels climbing the ladder to heaven. Their
mission, however, was more down-to-earth. They were the

troubleshooters who kept the pumps going.

Even though the town benefited from the government's open policy of homesteading the land, not all the inhabitants were pleased with the number of *gringos* who had moved in. They feared that the Americans would strip the land, take what profit they could, and leave behind worthless property. They had dealt in the past with "wildcatters" who escaped their responsibilities by moving on when money ran out or they tired of the job.

Chad and Luke were fortunate, then, to have the company of Reymundo, who was able to assure the doubtful residents that Chad Rush was honorable and trustworthy, and that he was dealing not only with the Mexican government, but with the large oil company in the area. For this reason Chad had been able to assure Manda of his safety when he joined the family at Christmas time.

True to his promise, Chad had not concerned himself with the affairs of government or political views of the people who worked for him or lived in the town. Along with Reymundo, he and Luke put in long days, attended the chapel services on Sunday, and otherwise kept to themselves. They never visited the taverns that lined the dirt street of Ocampo, nor did they listen to the gossip and rumors that flew about town.

It was surprising, then, that word of the latest political uprising reached them before the oil company had an opportunity to inform them.

"I heard news of trouble northeast of here," Reymundo reported. "I happened to be standing near two oil men who didn't know that I understood English. It is not good."

Chad and Luke waited for him to continue.

"Some Mexican revolutionaries have plundered and burned an American town just over the border in New Mexico. Your president has sent a general to find the leader, but the leader has fled back to Chihuahua."

"This is serious," Chad agreed. "I'm sure we will be hearing more about it soon."

He was right. The week wasn't over before they received notice that Americans were advised to leave Mexican territory as soon as possible.

"I must stay until I've settled my business," Chad told the men, "but the family should go at once." He looked worried. "Ethan is a level-headed boy, but I'm not sure that he can handle that much responsibility."

After considering several plans, the men decided that Reymundo would stay with Chad, and Luke would return to Galeana to escort the family to El Paso.

"They will be safe there until I'm able to join them," Chad decided. "I'm sure they would come to no harm in Galeana, but we should do as the government directs."

"It's Luke!" Simon's announcement brought everyone running to the doorway. For a long moment no one said anything, then everyone began talking at once.

"What are you doing here?"

"Where is Chad?"

"Is something wrong?"

"Is Papa all right?"

Luke waited until things quieted down before he answered. "I can only tell you one thing at a time. Sit down, and I'll explain why I'm here."

Manda sat down at the table. "Something has happened to Chad," she said. "Tell me."

"No, Chad is fine. He and Reymundo are working as usual. He sent me here with a message."

"The mail isn't going anymore?" Polly said. "That's a long way to come with a message."

"The United States government wants all Americans to leave Mexico. I came to take you out. As soon as the business of the land is taken care of, Chad will be along. There's nothing to worry about."

There was a stunned silence in the room.

"Is there danger here?" Manda was alarmed. "How soon do we have to go?"

"I don't think we're in danger," Luke replied, "and we don't have to leave tonight. I'll get a wagon in the morning while you pack. We can be ready to go after the noon meal."

"The noon meal! Tomorrow?" Polly was indignant. "Do you remember how long it took us to get ready to come here?"

Luke nodded. "I know. You'll have time to pack your clothes and bedding. The rest will have to stay. If Chad has time to get it on his way through, he will."

Manda looked around the room at the bright rugs and wall hangings they had acquired. She thought of the colorful pottery that would look so cheerful in her South

Dakota home. Surprisingly, she was going to miss this country of friendly people, *posadas*, marketplaces, and *fiesta* days. Mostly, she would miss her church friends, especially Carlotta.

As though she heard what Manda was thinking, Polly stated, "I ain't leaving here without saying good-bye to Carlotta. Will can run over and get her in the morning."

Long after the family had gone to bed, Ethan lay awake, looking out the small window over his bed. There would be no chance to say good-bye to Carlos, he was sure. He wished there were something he could leave for his friend. He knew that Carlos would come to the house to find out why Ethan didn't come to work.

Ethan was almost asleep when he knew what he could do. Quietly he slipped out of bed and lit a candle. Pulling his drawing book from under the cot, he quickly began to sketch. An hour later his gift was ready, and he fell asleep.

The next morning began before daybreak. Carlotta arrived and, amid tears, helped the ladies roll and tie the bedding and pile clothing in boxes. Polly and Frances packed baskets with food, and Simon was dispatched to buy fruit for the journey. Luke and Ethan loaded everything into the wagon.

Shortly after noon the family pulled away from the home they had come to love. Carlotta watched them head toward town. In her hand she held several pages of Ethan's drawing book, which she had promised to deliver to Carlos. Now she looked at the pictures Ethan had sketched. There was the little house they had just left. One page showed scenes of the village market, the burros carrying food or hay or baskets. Another was a picture of a bright fire and boys gathered around it.

Carlotta pondered over the last page. A large, two-story house stood beside a river. Cottonwood trees lined the yard. In the distance were some buffalo. On the bottom Ethan had written, *Mi casa in South Dakota. Come and visit me.*

There is little chance that Carlos or any of the other boys will ever leave this village, Carlotta thought sadly. *Ethan has been good for them.* She was glad that the family had come to Galeana.

As the wagon progressed through the marketplace, Ethan looked carefully down each side street, hoping to see one of his friends. There was no one in sight. These were the hours of *siesta*, and even the market booths were empty.

Polly, too, had hoped to see the *señoras* she visited with as she shopped. "I can't decide whether I'll miss getting out every day to walk to the market or be glad that I have food in the springhouse and cellar," she commented.

Manda nodded. "It will take a while to get used to staying at home most of the time. Of course there's more to take care of in the big house than we've had here." She sighed. "You know, I thought I'd be so glad to be going home that I wouldn't think of looking back. But I believe I'm going to be homesick for this little town. Luke, do you think the president is right? Is it dangerous for Americans to be here? We haven't seen any revolutionaries or bandits around Galeana."

"I think the president is being cautious," Luke replied. "Americans have been attacked in parts of Mexico, and some people have been killed. We're asked to leave because the government can't protect United States citizens if there is an uprising somewhere in the country. And they never know where it will be."

"It won't be here today," Simon declared. "There isn't even a burro on the road for as far as we can see."

Simon appeared to be right. The countryside was quiet under the afternoon sun. Even the small ranches they passed looked deserted. Although he wouldn't say anything to the others, Luke was a bit uneasy. He hadn't let on how urgent the request had been that all Americans leave as soon as possible. As he glanced at the mountains to the left of them, he recalled Chad's parting words.

"Watch carefully as you travel north. It's in those mountains that the rebel general is said to be holed up. He's protected by the people, because they love him. But his men are ruthless. They could decide not to let strangers go on to the border. You will be in our prayers. God be with you."

The sun was beginning to set when they stopped to eat the lunch Frances and Polly had prepared.

"If I'd had a little more warning, I could've baked yesterday," Polly grumbled. "But I suppose we can get bread wherever we stop tonight."

"I don't think we'll be stopping," Luke said. "I'd like to get into El Paso as soon as possible. If we keep right on the road, we should be in Texas before noon tomorrow. We'll rest the horses a few hours as soon as it gets dark, then we'll go on."

"You'd think we was being chased," Polly said. "All we've seen in this country is friendly people, and you're rushing us away like they was after us."

The younger children were asleep when the wagon returned to the deserted road later that evening. Ethan sat beside Luke and watched as the stars appeared in the cloudless sky. The breeze was cool, and he pulled his jacket tighter around his shoulders.

"It seems like we've been in Mexico longer than seven months, doesn't it?" Luke said.

"Yep. It was a long winter. You did a good job looking after the family."

"I'm glad to be going back," Ethan said. "We'll be home in time to help Henry with the planting. Did Chad write and say that we're coming?"

"Didn't have time. I'll send Henry a card from El Paso."

"How long will we stay in Texas?"

"If Chad isn't there by the first of next week, we'll go on. He hoped to be ready to leave soon after I did."

They rode the next hour in silence. Ethan was beginning to feel sleepy, but he wanted to stay awake to keep Luke company.

"There's a fire in the mountains ahead," Luke said softly.

They watched carefully as the light seemed to jump from place to place on the rugged hillside.

"Should we go on?" Ethan whispered.

"Got no choice. This is the only road. If it's an ambush,

they'll keep coming. We'll trust God to go with us."

The chill Ethan felt had nothing to do with the night air. These were rebels, probably bandits! He looked back at the others in the wagon. Manda and Polly were sitting up and looking toward the mountains.

"We don't have anything they'd want back here," Manda said quietly. "If they demand your money belt, Luke, give it to them."

Luke nodded. Having heard some stories of revenge against Americans in New Mexico, he feared for the safety of the women and children. Thankfully, he could pray, and he did so as they continued slowly toward the lights. It wasn't long until horses and men with fiery torches surrounded the wagon, and Luke was forced to stop.

"Stay quiet," Luke said to the others. "We'll be all right."

He tried to sound calmer than he felt. The shouting men and blazing fire made a frightening picture in the dark night. There was no way to tell how many were in the group, nor could anyone tell what their intentions might be. The ladies huddled together with Alice and the boys between them. The flames cast eerie shadows around the wagon, and Manda prayed that they would not be harmed.

"*Americanos!*" one man shouted, and the others seemed to push in closer. Ethan's heart sank as he thought of the people who had been kind to them, and the boys whose friendships he had won before they left Galeana. He hadn't even imagined meeting enemies of his people.

Suddenly from the midst of the crowd, a strong voice called out, "*Pare!*" At once the horses and men surrounding them began to back away. Ethan peered through the flickering flames and smoke, and dimly he could make out the large man who had issued the order.

It was General Villa! Ethan recognized him in the light of the torches the men held. The general's gaze moved from Ethan to the rest of the family and back to Ethan. He nodded and raised his hand, speaking a word to the other riders.

Ethan looked at Polly. She, too, had recognized the leader. She put her hand over her mouth, and her eyes were wide. General Villa spoke again, turned, and disappeared into the darkness. One by one the other riders followed him until only two horsemen remained. One of them spoke to Luke.

"*Adelante*."

Slowly the wagon went forward, and the road ahead looked as peaceful as it had been before they stopped. It seemed as though they might have dreamed the events of the last few minutes, except for the presence of the two riders on either side of the wagon. No one dared to speak until, several miles down the road, the men stopped and then motioned for Luke and the wagon to continue.

"*Gracias*," Luke said.

The men nodded, then turned and rode swiftly into the hills. For several moments, no one spoke.

Then, "Whatever was that all about?" Manda said. "Ethan, that man looked at you as though he knew you."

Ethan and Polly exchanged a look.

"You tell, Polly," Ethan said. "You met General Villa first."

"That was Pancho Villa?" Manda gasped. "And you met him? How? Where? Why didn't you tell us about it?"

"I didn't know who he was then," Polly replied. "I thought he looked like a bandit, but he treated me real good. He was a kind man who helped me find my way back to the road from town. Ethan came looking for me and met up with us."

"He was nice to me, too," said Ethan. "He said we had something in common because he was an orphan and had a sister to look after. He told me about the newspaper job. I ran into him a couple more times after that."

Polly shook her head. "Ma would spin in her grave if she knew I'd let a general in the Mexican Revolution carry my groceries home for me."

"I wouldn't have rested easy in my bed either, if I'd known that my family was hobnobbing with the most famous outlaw in Mexico," Manda declared. "I still don't know why in the world he paid any attention to Ethan."

Now that the danger was past, the children began to chatter about their frightening experience. Ethan only half listened to them. God knew that Polly's chance meeting with Pancho Villa and their later friendship would result in all their lives being spared. Was it possible that God knew every event of Ethan's life, and was directing him each day? As the daylight grew stronger and they neared the border crossing, Ethan decided that it was not only possible, but very probable. Whatever lay ahead in life for him, God was already there!

LOOKING TOWARD
THE FUTURE

The border crossing between El Paso, Texas, and Juarez, Mexico, was forbidden territory to the younger children. Their protests went unheeded by Manda.

"We didn't leave Mexico to be shot in Texas," she said. "Those bullets have no idea which side of the border you're on. You may play in the park when Frances has time to go with you, or you can go walking with Luke. I'm not going to turn you loose and risk having to look for you when your papa gets here."

"When is he coming?"

Manda sighed. "Just as soon as he can. You're no more anxious than I am to get on the train for home."

Polly looked out the hotel window at the busy street below. "We've been here three days. If Chad and Reymundo started soon after Luke left, they should be here by the first of the week. You planning to wait for them?"

Manda nodded. "I don't want to go back to South Dakota without Chad. I suppose I could send Luke and Frances on with the children, but I'd feel better if we're all together."

Ethan was free to come and go as he pleased, and the border guards were soon familiar with the young boy who stood and anxiously watched the road that led to Juarez. Although the fighting had ceased, military units were still in evidence.

"Them rebels over there is staying holed up in the mountains," one of the men told Ethan. "Their general is a smart one. No one ever sees him, but he knows just what's going on over here. We'll never catch him if he don't want us to."

Ethan was thankful for that, but he didn't say so. He just listened and watched.

Ocampo went about business as usual on the surface, but behind the bustle of activity lay a feeling of unrest. When Luke left to escort the family out of the country, Chad expressed relief.

"I feel better knowing that they are on the way home," he said. "Luke will look after things as well as I could. Now we need to settle up here and be on our way."

"Settling up" wasn't as easy as he had hoped. There were many buyers ready to take advantage of the fact that the *Americanos* were being forced out of the country and were in no position to wait for the best offer.

"If I were you, I would deal directly with your American

oil company," Reymundo advised him. "They will be required to leave, and the government will protect them. You should get a fair price."

Chad didn't get the profit he had planned on, but he felt that the trip had been reasonably successful.

"We'd have done better if we'd been allowed to stay the full year, but it happened to be the wrong time for this venture. At least we didn't lose everything, and we have something to go back to."

The journey back to Galeana was uneventful. Carlotta had completed the packing of things that Manda wanted but couldn't take with her. And church friends had advice for the men.

"The northern mountain area isn't safe for travelers," they told Chad. "The rebels are stopping wagons and searching them. Many things, they take. You may not get to the border with your goods."

"Have they harmed the people?"

"Not that we've heard. But it is a terrifying experience to be stopped on the road and surrounded by bandits."

In spite of the reports, Chad was anxious to continue on to El Paso. Although he had given Luke instructions to take the family on home if he didn't appear, he was sure that Manda would not want to go without him. It was decided that an old mule-driven wagon piled high with hay would be less likely to attract attention. If they were stopped, they would appear to be two farmers on the road to Juarez.

The wagon was loaded, and the church people prayed for their safety. It was late afternoon before Reymundo and

Chad left Galeana and headed north. Again, the road was deserted. Their progress was slower than Luke's had been, since the elderly burro wasn't inclined to make the trip at all, let alone at a reasonable pace. The men resigned themselves to a long, plodding trek with very little change of scenery.

"We'd better stop a few hours," Reymundo suggested "or this animal will refuse to move at all. We can go on after dark."

They ate the food Carlotta had prepared for them, then rested until the sun was out of sight. In the distance the mountains loomed on their left, and the men watched them until darkness fell.

"I will lift up mine eyes unto the hills, from whence cometh my help. My help cometh from the Lord, which made heaven and earth." Chad quoted the first two verses of Psalm 121 softly, and felt comfort from the thought that they were under God's protection.

Reymundo, too, had been thinking about the hours that lay ahead. "He will give His angels charge over you, to guard you in all your ways," he said. "I believe that we will be safe, no matter what lies before us."

Nevertheless, when they were stopped by a group of soldiers the next morning as the sun came up, Chad's heart pounded with fear. Even though he looked as much like a farmer as Reymundo did, Chad knew that he couldn't pass as a Mexican citizen. He would have to admit that he was an American if they inquired. But the questions the men asked were not what the travelers expected.

"Where are you going?"

"To Juarez, *Señor*," Reymundo replied.

"You will stay there?"

Reymundo paused a moment. "No, *Señor*. I will go on with my friend to El Paso. Then I will return."

The soldier looked sharply at Chad.

"Where do you come from?"

"I have come today from Galeana," he replied. "I will join my family in El Paso, then continue on to South Dakota."

The man turned to one of his companions and said, "This is the one. He is here."

Turning back to Reymundo, he gave him rapid directions, and Reymundo turned the wagon toward the mountain and followed the soldiers.

"What did he say? Where are we going? Was he talking about me?"

Reymundo nodded. "Yes. He says you are to see the general."

The general? Chad's heart sank as he imagined what might happen to them. What had he done? Was there a problem about the money he was taking from the country?

The small building before which they stopped seemed like a long way from the road, but they had reached it sooner than Chad was ready to see it. He was relieved to find that Reymundo would be going in with him. Two soldiers accompanied them, and they were escorted into a room furnished only with a desk and chair. A dark-haired man with heavy eyebrows and a drooping mustache sat behind the desk. He regarded the two men silently for what seemed like a long time. Finally he spoke to Reymundo in Spanish.

"Was your work in Ocampo a success?"

"*Sí*, General."

"You are escorting your companion to the border?"

"*Sí*."

The general nodded, then looked at Chad. Although Chad's knees were shaking, his eyes never left the general's face. Many thoughts crowded his mind as he stood there. It was possible that he would be taken captive; many others had been. Undoubtedly they would take the money he carried. If he escaped with his life, Chad would be grateful.

Suddenly the general reached into his pocket, drew out a heavy object, and laid it on the desk.

"Ethan's key!" Chad exclaimed. "Where is he? Do you have Ethan here? Is my family—?"

"No, *Señor*. Your son is not here. Your family has had a safe passage to El Paso." He looked at the object before him. "I am reluctant to let it go, but the key must be returned to Ethan. I have never received a greater token of friendship. I want him to know that it is being returned to him in the same spirit." The big man stood up. "Take care of that boy. You don't know what great fortune you had when he came into your life. You may go now."

Chad and Reymundo were escorted back to the road, and the soldiers disappeared into the hills. As the little mule plodded along toward Juarez, Chad puzzled over the last hour's events. *Of all that had occurred during their stay in*

Mexico, he thought, *this was the strangest incident of all*.

After several miles, Reymundo's voice broke into Chad's thoughts. "I think we have a problem. Hold the reins while I check."

For the first time, Chad was aware that the wagon was tipping perilously. Reymundo jumped down from the slow-moving vehicle and inspected the rear wheel.

"It's coming off," he informed Chad. "We won't make it to the border in this wagon. We wanted to look like poor farmers? We couldn't have done much better than this."

It was now the middle of morning, and clouds were gathering over the foothills. There was a storm approaching, and a glance in both directions revealed no other conveyance or person on the road.

"We can't just stand here and soak up the rain," Reymundo said. "I'll load the burro with as much as he'll take, and we'll carry what we can. I'd rather be walking than wasting time alongside the road."

It was soon apparent that the burro didn't share his preference. He dug in his heels and refused to move. Pulling and pushing had very little effect.

"This doesn't look too promising," Chad said. "We'll have to leave what we can't carry and go on without him, unless the Lord sees fit to move him."

At that moment lightning struck the earth near them. A clap of thunder shook the ground. Chad and Reymundo dived under the wagon. The sky opened up as rain and hail pelted the earth. Reymundo watched the burro high-tail it down the road, his ears back and his hooves flying.

"I guess we'd better chase him before he's out of sight," Reymundo grumbled. "When the Lord moves something, He doesn't waste any motion."

By the time the men caught up with the burro, the animal was winded and willing to be led slowly toward Juarez.

Dinner at the hotel the following noon was a quiet and sober meal. Manda and Luke had agreed that they should not wait any longer for Chad, but take the late afternoon train north.

"If you want to stay in Willow Creek until he comes, Ethan and I can go on by train," Luke suggested. "I'd like to be home to help Henry with the planting. The rest of you can come on in the wagon when Chad arrives."

Thus it was decided, and a letter was left at the desk for Chad, outlining the plan. Polly was overjoyed at the thought of being on the way home.

"I hope this trip has taken all the wander out of Chad's foot," she declared. "I'll be happy to spend the rest of my days on the plains looking at the cottonwood trees and cooking for my family."

"You'd have felt terrible if you'd missed this trip, Polly, and you know it," Luke told her.

Polly admitted it. "Yes, I would have. Nobody could ever tell you about the things we saw and tasted and smelled so's you could really know what it was like. And imagine not knowing Carlotta and the other people at the church."

"We all made good friends there," Manda said, "but I'm

glad to be going home. I just wish Chad had gotten here in time to go with us. What if he doesn't get to the border? What if they're stopped by the soldiers and not allowed to leave the country?"

Will had left the table and was standing by the big front window. Now he called out, "He's here, Mama!"

Ethan stood up to look. "No, Will, that's not him. He and Reymundo are coming in a wagon. Those men just have an old burro."

Luke walked to the window. "Chad wouldn't come into town with a week's beard and clothes like that. Those fellows look like they were caught in a— Well, what do you know? It *is* Chad!"

The next day Reymundo hired a wagon and prepared to head back to Mexico.

"I'll miss you, *mi amígo*," he said to Chad.

"And I, you," Chad replied. "I couldn't have successfully completed my business without your help. It's easy to make mistakes in another country and offend the people, and without your help, I would have done so. The Lord be with you as you travel back to Galeana."

The family was ready to board the train that evening. At breakfast, Chad pulled the key from his pocket and handed it to Ethan. "A friend of yours gave this to me, Ethan."

Then the whole story had to be told all over again, and Chad relayed his adventure too.

"I never expected to get the key back," Ethan said. "How did he know you were the one to give it to?"

"The soldiers said they questioned everyone who passed there in the days after you went by. That's the reason General Villa has remained safe—he knows what's going on around him. He also has a good place to stay. I don't think I could find my way back to his hideout if I wanted to."

"I don't think I'd want to," Luke said. "I'm glad to be on this side of the border."

When the train left El Paso that evening, the whole family was glad to leave their adventures behind them and head back to the plains.

"Amelia will have the garden in, and we'll be just in time to can the early beans and peas," Polly said. "Won't that kitchen look good?"

"I'll be tending my flowers," Manda said happily. "I know I'll miss the cactuses, but I can't wait to see the lilacs and roses."

Polly reached under the seat and pulled out a cloth bag. "You won't miss the cactuses. I brought some along. I figured since they growed like weeds, nobody would miss a few."

"I brought something, too," Frances said. "Carlotta gave me a lace *mantilla*. I don't know where I'll wear it, but I can show it to the children at school in the fall."

"I've got my *sombrero*," Will announced, "and I am going to wear it!"

It seemed that everyone had brought something home to remind them of Mexico, except Luke.

"I couldn't carry what I wanted to bring," Luke said glumly.

"What was that, Luke?"

"An oil well."

The scenery didn't seem to fly by as swiftly going home as it had when they had traveled south. Ethan watched out the window absently and thought of the little town they had left. Its crooked streets and empty warehouses were as clear in his memory as though he were still there. Even though he might never again see Carlos or the other fellows, they wouldn't be forgotten. He could hear Chad and Luke discussing the crops, and Manda and Polly talking about the house and garden. Everyone had plans for the year ahead.

When the train steamed into Willow Creek, Ben and Lydia Archer were the first people they saw. Manda greeted her friend with delight, then looked around at the others who had gathered to welcome them.

"My, your children have gotten big," Edith Watkins exclaimed. "I believe Will is as tall as Ethan was when they first came here."

Will is a year older than I was, Ethan thought. *He's almost nine*. Then suddenly, Ethan remembered. It had been just six years ago today that the Coopers had first set foot on this platform. Many of these same people had been here then, wanting to look over the orphans and perhaps take one home. What a lot had happened since then!

Not all of it, Ethan reflected, had been happy. Chad had been a harsh taskmaster.

"He treats you boys like his pa treated him," Polly once said to Ethan. "I ain't saying it's the best way to raise a young 'un, but Chad's become a successful man. Folks ain't ever going to understand him, but they respect him."

He's the only father I've had, Ethan thought, *and I've learned a lot from him. I'm thankful for a home where I can keep the others with me. I hope all the orphans on that train are as well off as we are.*

Someone poked Ethan on the shoulder, and he whirled around to find a grinning Bert standing behind him. They greeted each other joyfully with much pounding on the back and playful shoving.

"I didn't think I'd see you this time," Ethan said. "Luke and Polly and I are going on home with the evening train. Chad is staying to drive the wagon and the rest of the family back."

"Would I miss being here today of all days?"

"You remembered what date it was, then."

"No, but Mama did. She celebrates it every year, just like our birthdays. It kind of sneaks up on me. We've been so busy, what with a new baby and all. Wait until you see my sister. She looks just like me!" Bert laughed happily at his joke. "I'm kidding. She looks like Mama. And it's a good thing, too."

By the time the late train arrived, their plans were made to leave for school as soon as the harvest was over. Luke, Polly, and Ethan settled into their seats for the final lap of the journey.

"I've made my last trip bouncing across the country in a wagon," Polly declared. "My bones can't take anymore. I don't want to go across the country again unless I can fly!"

"Looks like you're homebound then," Luke said. "You're never going to fly till you go to heaven."

The summer passed quickly for the family. Henry and Amelia moved into their new home, and between them, Amelia and Polly kept the farm hands well fed. Everyone worked at something, even Will, who celebrated his ninth birthday in June.

All too soon for Manda, fall arrived, and with it school. Frances would teach in Winner, and the younger children would go in with her each day. Ethan, though still torn between his desire to learn and his reluctance to leave the place where he felt secure and cared for, was ready to leave for Kansas.

He looked back as the wagon carried him down the road toward the train depot. The others were waving to him. Simon, almost eleven and nearly as tall as Ethan; Alice, a young lady at twelve; Will, no longer the chubby baby that Ethan had been responsible for. All the rest of the family were lined up at the fence to watch him leave too. Ethan waved to them, then turned to look down the road toward the future. Luke slapped the reins on Ben's back, and another chapter of the orphan's journey began.

What lay ahead? Ethan didn't know, but he was sure that God was going with him, just as He had from the beginning of the trip.

EPILOGUE

The real "Ethan" died at the age of ninety-six, before
this book was finished. I was pleased to be able to present
Looking for Home and *Whistle-stop West* to him several
months before that. He looked at them carefully, then said,
"My, my. Who would have thought anyone would ever
write a book about me?"

I could not have chosen a better subject. During the
four years that the books were in process, I grew to love and
admire Ethan the child, and the man I learned so much
about through his family.

If Ethan was surprised that his life could be the subject
of a book, those who knew him and his family were not.
Ethan married a lovely young lady whom he met at a
Christian college. Together they had four sons and twin
daughters, now teachers, business people, and missionaries.
They in turn have raised children to honor the Lord. There
is every reason to believe that the influence of this godly
man will continue on through succeeding generations.

Although Ethan remembered much about his early life,
the Orphan Train, and his adopted family, many of the
details were left to my imagination. His children recognize a

number of the incidents retold, and have been gracious enough to agree that the story has not strayed so far from the truth as to be pure fiction.

Of particular interest to me was the time the family spent in Mexico. The circumstances leading to the home-steading for oil, which drew Chad Rush to the country, did occur. The events surrounding Pancho Villa and the revolutionaries actually took place over a period of several years, rather than in the few months portrayed in the story. Ethan did remember seeing the infamous general who later, as Pancho Villa predicted in the story, was assassinated by his own men.

Is there a story in every life, no matter how unimportant it seems to the one living it? Indeed there is. Those of us who believe that God has a design for every day as we follow Him will find our years more exciting than anything a novelist will ever imagine!

Arleta Richardson
1996